Witty TENALIRAMA

Amusing questions, funny answers, tricky problems, witty solutions—all put together for your entertainment.

Compiled by
'KUNWAR' ANIL KUMAR

Edited by
SHRUTI SRIVASTAVA

MANOJ PUBLICATIONS

Publishers

Manoj Publications

761, Main Road, Burari, Delhi-110084

Ph: 27611349, 27611116, Fax : 27611546,

Mobile : 9868112194

E-mail : info@manojpublications.com

Website : www.manojpublications.com

Showroom :

Manoj Publications

1583-84, Dariba Kalan, Chandni Chowk, Delhi-6

Phone : 23262174, 23268216, Mobile : 9818753569

ISBN : 978-81-8133-475-6

Price : 80/-

Seventh Edition : 2010

Printers
Jai Maya Offset
Jhilmil Industrial Area, Delhi-110095

Witty Tenalirama : 'Kunwar' Anil Kumar

WHO WAS TENALI RAMAKRISHNA

Tenali Ramakrishna, or more popularly known as Tenali Ram, is not a concocted character in the history of Karnataka. He did exist, and existed with all his might of wits and wisdom. He led his way and made it possible for himself to be appointed as court jester at the court of Krishna Dev Rai, using his wits and wisdom and presence of mind. King Krishna Dev Rai was the ruler of Vijayanagar, who, with the help of his capable administration, had made Vijayanagar the most powerful kingdom of Karnataka.

Tenali Ramakrishna held the same status in the eyes of King Krishna Dev Rai as Birbal had in the eyes of Emperor Akbar. The only difference was that Birbal was one of the nine gems of Emperor Akbar and Tenali Ramakrishna was one of the eight gems of King Krishna Dev Rai. The courtiers of King Krishna Dev Rai were just as jealous of Tenali Ramakrishna as were the courtiers of Emperor Akbar jealous of Birbal. The courtiers at the court of King Krishna Dev Rai always looked for an opportunity to let Tenali Ramakrishna down in the eyes of the King. But Tenali Ramakrishna was so witty that he would not only make their designs fail, rather he would attain more nearness to the king and bag a handsome reward as well. The stories of Tenali Ramakrishna are not only entertaining, they also give us knowledge and teach us ethics. These stories are historical assets of our country and make us aware of the political, economic, social and religious situation of fifteenth-sixteenth century.

Tenali Ramakrishna was the son of a poor Brahmin—Ishwar Prasad Ramaiya. The real name of Tenali Ramakrishna was Ramalinga. He was born in a small town, Galipadu, of Guntur district. But it is said that his father died when he was only three days old. He was taken care of by his maternal uncle who lived in a small town, Tenali. Ramalinga had a sharp brain ever since his childhood. All his comrades acknowledged his supremacy.

Tenali Ramakrishna had a wish to go to the court of Krishna Dev. Rai and offer his services. And he also succeeded in fulfilling his wish. But the status Tenali Ramakrishna enjoyed at the King's court, was not attained by him just like that; he really had to struggle for it.

Tenali Ramakrishna was a man of firm determination. And it was because of this determination and self-confidence that he could make a place for himself at the King's court. Though there are thousands of stories of Tenali Ramakrishna, we have carefully selected a few which are entertaining and give us knowledge, and also teach us ethics.

—**Publishers**

CONTENTS

*A grand show of wit, presence of mind,
mental alertness and one-up manship*

1

BLESSED BY GODDESS KALI

Karnataka, ruled by so many dynasties, had its golden period under the rule of King Krishna Dev Rai of Vijayanagara kingdom. He was brave and powerful, and exercised great control over his administration to keep his subjects happy and prosperous. He was also a great admirer of art, culture, and literature. And it was only under his rule that these things touched great heights of accomplishment.

King Krishna Dev Rai had eight wise ministers at his royal court, and were popularly known as eight diggajas* (eight elephants). Tenali Ramakrishna was one of these eight ministers at the royal court. He

* The literal meaning of Diggaja according to our mythology is—'a legendary elephant which had eight faces and carried earth on its head.'

was mainly a jester and was loved and admired by King Krishna Dev Rai for his witty jests. But this was all with the blessing of goddess Kali that he became a jester and gained popularity.

The story goes thus—

There was a village 'Tenali' which had a big temple of goddess Kali on its outskirts. Ramakrishna, a Brahmin boy of Tenali village, used to come to this temple everyday to offer his worships to goddess Kali. He was a bright boy with sparkling eyes. He was soft-splken and well-behaved.

One afternoon, as he sat in meditation after having had bath in a nearby pond, a sage happened to pass by. He saw so young a boy sitting in meditation and was filled with admiration for him. He was greatly impressed. The sage came and sat quietly by his side.

He spoke to him after his meditation was over—

"O dear child! I am impressed indeed to see you meditating at this age. Is it that you come to this temple everyday?"

"Yes, Swamiji! I come here everyday," said Ramakrishna innocently.

"Do you have true reverence for goddess Kali?" asked the sage again.

"Yes, Swamiji! I do have. And I am also aware that she takes care of me," said Ramakrishna.

"If that be so, you must have seen her also," said the sage with a smile, pouring all his affection.

"No, Swamiji!" said Ramakrishna innocently. "She has never appeared before me," and then looking at the sage with curious eyes, he said, "Can I see her?"

"Of course you can, my child," said the sage still smiling. "Are you not a devotee of goddess Kali? Isn't she like a mother to you? All that you have to do, if you really wish her to appear before you, is to sit in meditation with full concentration for one whole night. Pleased with your devotion and worship she will appear before you and shower her kind blessings on you. Gods and goddesses never disappoint their true devotees. But you should not get frightened when you see her."

"But why should I get frightened to see her? She is like my mother. I offer my worships to her everyday," said Ramakrishna.

The sage was mighty pleased to hear the young Brahmin boy. "All right! I give you a mantra, continuous repetition of which, for one full night, will serve your purpose," saying this the sage left.

Ramakrishna was so resolute a boy with unshakeable faith that without caring to assuage his hunger and quench his thirst, he sat down in meditation the same night and began uttering the mantra given by the sage.

He was so lost in his prayer and repetition of mantra that he could not realise that the night was over and the sun had risen.

Suddenly he heard a sweet voice calling him—

* a poet who is impregnable and can compose poem on any subject without any difficulty.

"Ramakrishna! Ramakrishna! Open your eyes. See I am here before you, my child."

Ramakrishna opened his eyes and saw goddess Kali before him. But he never expected her to appear with a thousand faces. What he saw was the form of goddess Kali with a thousand faces, all having red and gleaming eyes; but she had only two arms.

Seeing goddess Kali, in such a strange form, made Ramakrishna burst into laughter. He was not at all frightened.

But goddess Kali became furious. "Ramakrishna," she said, "What is it that makes you laugh? Do you have no fearing tissues? Are you not afraid of me?"

"O mother! Why should I be afraid of you? Are children supposed to be afraid of their mothers? Moreover, I am your devotee; I offer my worships to you everyday without fail, and with true reverence for you. There is no reason why I should be afraid of you," said Ramakrishna very innocently.

"I am aware that you are not afraid of me, but you owe me an explanation. Tell me what made you laugh at me," said goddess Kali.

"Mother! Your thousand faces and only two arms, a combination which is totally out of proportion, made me laugh," said Ramakrishna.

"Why do you find it out of proportion?" said goddess Kali.

"Because, you see mother, we have only one face and two arms; but when we have a running nose, it sometimes becomes very difficult to manage with two hands. And in your case, God forbid, if you catch cold and have a thousand running noses, it will become impossible for you to manage," said Ramakrishna with such simplicity that goddess Kali forgot her anger and began laughing.

The childlike innocence and simplicity of Ramakrishna filled goddess Kali with great affection for him.

12

"Ramakrishna! I am happy indeed. Your devotion for me, your simplicity and innocence has greatly impressed me. I grant you a boon and bless you to become a jester and make everyone laugh," said goddess Kali. "Go to Vijayanagar, which is ruled by King Krishna Dev Rai; present yourself at his court. From now you will be known as 'Vikatkavi'*."

Having blessed Ramakrishna goddess Kali disappeared.

Ramakrishna remained there for hours, lost in the thoughts of goddess Kali. It took him a long time to make himself believe that goddess Kali had actually appeared in physical form before him.

After some time he left the place and headed for Vijayanagara without knowing what the future had in its womb for him. But this was the instance that made a foundation for him to be known as 'Tenali Ramakrishna' or 'Tenali Ram' in future.

2

RAMAKRISHNA EXPLOITS HIS WITS

Tenali Ramakrishna reached the palace's gate, but the guards wouldn't let him in. Being a stranger he was not allowed entry. He began thinking—

"How strange! Goddess Kali sends me here and these guards won't let me in. How to manage the situation?" Then Tenali Ramakrishna thought—"But goddess Kali has blessed me to become a jester; and a jester must be witty. All right! I must apply my wits," thinking thus he suddenly saw a troupe of artistes going towards the palace. Tenali Ramakrishna was quick to learn from their conversation that they were professional artists and had been allowed to give performance before the King. One of them, who was perhaps their chief, was heard saying—

"I have visited so many kings but none like King Krishna Dev Rai. What I feel happy about is that he understands art and literature and also rewards suitably."

All the other artistes nodded in agreement.

Quick witted Tenali Ramakrishna immediately thought of a plan. Hiding himself from the eyes of the guards, he went behind the fence that surrounded the palace and changed his dress; he also did a little of make-up to make himself look like a shepherd. Now once again he approached the guards, and again he was denied entry.

"Look! I too am a member of the troupe of artistes. It took me a little time to give a final touch to my make-up; and hence I am late. My fellow artistes have already gone in. Kindly allow me," said Tenali Ramakrishna almost pleadingly.

"But we cannot allow just anyone. You will not be allowed entry," said one of the guards with a cunning smile.

Tenali Ramakrishna could easily grasp the meaning of this cunning smile.

Quick-witted as he was, he too wore a smile on his face and said, "Sir, please! I shall indeed be very grateful to you if you let me in. I have heard King Krishna Dev Rai is very kind and generous, and rewards suitably. I shall let you have half of whatever reward I get, if you kindly allow me to go in."

The guard thought for a while and then the allurement of half of the award got the better of him. He permitted Tenali Ramakrishna to go in.

This was for the first time ever in his life that Tenali Ramakrishna was entering a palace. He was dumbfounded to see the grandeur of everything all around. He was looking at everything wide-eyed. Bewildered by the grandeur, wearing a dazed expression on his face, he accidently stepped on to the stage where the artistes were giving their performance.

"Krishna Leela" was being enacted. And it was at this moment that Tenali Ramakrishna had made his entry and placed himself amidst Gopikas. The prompter and characters all got confused. This kind of entry was not there in the script. Gradually the truth began sinking in, and the artistes and the audience got to know the fact that it was a wrong entry.

The disruption caused by the wrong entry of Tenali Ramakrishna infuriated King Krishna Dev Rai terribly. The guards caught him and brought him almost dragging to the King.

"Tell me your identity. Who are you and what has prompted you to cause disruption in the enactment of drama?" said King Krishna Dev Rai frothing at the month.

"My Lord! My name is Ramakrishna and I am from the village— Tenali. I am a jester and I have come here to amuse you with my jests," said Tenali Ramakrishna.

"But who sent you here," asked the King still angry.

"My Lord! Goddess Kali sent me here. She blessed me to become a jester. Have I been able to please you, My Lord?" said Tenali Ramakrishna innocently.

"Yes, I am so happy with you that I am going to ask my guards to give you fifty lashes on your back. I think that's the only way you can be suitably rewarded. Will that suffice?" said King Krishna Dev Rai angrily.

"My Lord!" said Tenali Ramakrishna, "You are a king. Anything given by the king should be accepted happily by his subjects. But I have a problem, My Lord. I have promised one of your guards half the share of whatever reward I get. And it was only then that he allowed me entry. True to my word I must fulfil my promise."

King Krishna Dev Rai looked at Tenali Ramakrishna in disbelief. His anger had vanished. Now he began taking interest in Tenali Ramakrishna. In order to further test his wits the King said—

"But since you have bribed my guard, which is a cognizable offence, I award you a death punishment. You have managed to escape the punishment of lashes, but let me see how you escape the death sentence. You will be decapitated tomorrow morning.

The guards took him away and imprisoned him.

Everyone at the court was shocked to hear so severe a punishment for so ordinary an offence. But a king's order is after all a royal order. The courtiers were sad-stricken, but Tenali Ramakrishna had already begun applying his wits and thinking of a plan to save his life.

Next morning the guards came and took Tenali Ramakrishna out of the prison. While the guards were taking him away Tenali Ramakrishna was talking to them without any sign of nervousness on his face. He was absolutely normal. The guards were extremely surprised to see a person, under death sentence, so normal. They were feeling pity on him. But they were helpless. They had to carry out royal orders.

After they came out of the town and reached a river bank, Tenali Ramakrishna said—

"Dear fellows! you have the royal orders to decapitate me, and I am mentally prepared for it. But it would be so very kind of you if you kindly allow me to take a dip in the holy water of the river Tungabhadra. It is in our custom to take a bath before leaving this mortal body."

The guards debated this issue among themselves and then one of them said—

"Look dear! If it is in your custom to take a bath before dying, it is in our custom to allow the last wish of the person who is dying. We have nothing against you. But we are helpless, because we have to carry out royal orders. Please go and have a bath in the river."

Tenali Ramakrishna took bath in the river Tungabhadra, came out of it and sat in a clean place to meditate. He remained in meditation for a long time, and when he opened his eyes, he found that the guards were already preparing themselves to execute him. But he didn't lose courage. He said, "Dear guards! It has been indeed very kind of you to have allowed me my last wish. I am happy I have had a bath and offered my last prayers. In fact I have no right to ask for anything more; but believe me I am terribly hungry. Would you not allow a poor Brahmin to assuage his hunger before you put him to sleep permanently?"

Coming to know that the person they were going to behead was a Brahmin, filled the guards with a shudder of horror. This was for the first time in their lives that they were going to execute a Brahmin.

The guards discussed the matter among themselves. One of the guards said—

"Brother! We are being made to commit a great sin. You know what killing a Brahmin means? We shall all be sent to hell and tortured in many ways."

"But brother! We can also not disobey our King. We have to carry out his orders. But at least let us allow him to eat his fill," said the other guard.

The guards went and brought some fruits and a tender coconut and gave it to Tenali Ramakrishna to eat and assuage his hunger. He ate to his heart's content and then began yawning as if readying himself to take a wap. Within a short time Tenali Ramakrishna was deep asleep and snoring loudly. The guards were watching everything helplessly.

Tenali Ramakrishna woke up after having slept for hours together. He opened his eyes, looked around and then spoke in a very surprised tone—"Hey! How is it that my head is still on my shoulders? You haven't executed my yet? You should have decapitated me while I was asleep.

18

Anyway...it's still not too late. Come on, cut off my head, go and inform your king that you have carried out his orders."

The guards were relieved to quite an extent to hear him speak thus.

"All right! I understand your problem. Do one thing. I shall go into the river in neck deep water, and when I say 'Jai Shree Ram', you cut my head off," spoke Tenali Ramakrishna again.

The guards agreed and followed him into the river, and stood by his sides with bare swords in their hand. Tenali Ramakrishna closed his eyes and said 'Jai Shree Ram', but as soon as the guards waved their swords to chop off his head, he took a dip and swam away from there. The guards could only slice the air. They were dumbfounded as if some miracle had taken place. They began looking around and searching for him. Tenali Ramakrishna surfaced at quite a distance after some time.

"Look! You did try to behead me in trying to execute the orders of the King; but you failed. Now you please take me to the King, and I shall explain to him everything. Believe me, he won't be angry with you," said Tenali Ramakrishna.

The guards took him to King Krishna Dev Rai and narrated the whole sequence of happenings to him. The King was impressed indeed. But in order to put him to further tests he said, "You are fortunate that you managed to escape this time, but withdrawing the royal order is out of question." Then turning towards the guards he said, "Take this cunning guy to the outskirts of the town, bury him upto his neck and get his head trampled under the feet of an elephant. And take care to see that he doesn't manage to escape this time."

Despite having given such orders, King Krishna Dev Rai was sure that Tenali Ramakrishna would definitely manage to survive. In fact he was only trying to measure his wits. He had already begun liking him and was planning to appoint him as one of his ministers.

The guards took Tenali Ramakrishna away from the town, and after finding a suitable place, they dug a hole in the ground, deep enough to be able to bury him upto his neck. Having put him into the pit, they began filling the pit with the dug out clay.

Now there was no way Tenali Ramakrishna could come out of it and save himself from the hands of death.

The guards went away, leaving him alone in that position, to bring an elephant to have his head trampled.

Tenali Ramakrishna was as helpless as a mouse in a mousetrap. It was probably at this jittery stage of his life that he started worrying. He quickly began thinking of some possible way that might help him save his life. He was worriedly thinking thus when he happened to see a washerman passing by, carrying a heavy load of clothes on his back. The washerman had a large lump on his back. This was probably due to carrying heavy loads on his back. He was not able to walk straight.

Suddenly the washerman saw Tenali Ramakrishna buried upto his neck in the ground.

"O God! What strange people are there on earth," thought the washerman to himself. Then he said, "What the hell are you doing, young man? Why have you buried yourself?"

Quick witted Tenali Ramakrishna immediately thought of a plan and said, "Dear old man! Don't be surprised to see me in this position. I am in fact curing my hunchback. This was a problem that had made my life a hell. But now I am already feeling cured. I must thank the doctor who advised me to do so."

Now the washerman was looking wide-eyed at Tenali Ramakrishna, thinking if he too could take the same treatment and cure his hunchback.

"Can I also take the same treatment?" asked the washerman haltingly.

"Yes, why not? My doctor has gone to the town and will be back in another three hours from now. Either wait for the doctor for three hours, or help me come out of the pit, and you yourself get into it to straighten your back," said Tenali Ramakrishna.

But the washerman was getting impatient. Having known the remedy it was impossible for him to wait for another three long hours. The washerman helped Tenali Ramakrishna come out of the pit.

"See my back has become straight; there is no lump on it," said Tenali Ramakrishna.

The washerman looked at his back and was surprised to see that there was no trace of lump anywhere.

"Dear! I am getting into the pit. Please fill it up," said the washerman impatiently.

This is what Tenali Ramakrishna had wanted. Having buried the washerman upto his neck in his place, he disappeared from the scene with the bundle of clothes. The washerman was feeling happy that the lump on his back was going to be be cured, and Tenali Ramakrishna was happy that he had once again managed to survive.

Meanwhile the washerman saw two guards coming with an elephant. Within fraction of a moment everything became clear to him. He began pleading for his life as soon as the guards came near him with the elephant.

"Look sir! I don't understand why you want to kill me. What have I done?" said the nervous washerman.

The guards were looking at him with their mouths agape.

"Who are you? How did you get into this pit. We had buried another man," said one of the guards still not able to understand anything.

"I am a washerman," said the washerman, "and the person who was already buried here lured me into getting into this pit, saying that getting into the pit would cure the lump on my back. He also said that he himself had been advised by some doctor to cure his lump in this manner." The washerman paused for a moment and then said, "But now I understand what he was upto."

The guards also understood everything. They helped him get out of the pit and took him straight to the palace. When the guards reached the palace, Tenali Ramakrishna was already present there with the bundle of clothes. Seeing the washerman he explained everything to King Krishna Dev Rai. The King burst into laughter and congratulated Tenali Ramakrishna for applying his wits according to circumstances.

"I am indeed very much impressed by you," said the King, "I wish to appoint you as one of my ministers."

"Thank you very much, My Lord! I am feeling quite elated; but I have a problem. I have been blessed by goddess Kali to become a jester. I am afraid I shall not be able to carry out the responsibilities of a minister," said Tenali Ramakrishna.

Though Tenali Ramakrishna had spoken very humbly, King Krishna Dev Rai got infuriated once again.

"I don't accept even the slightest gesture of defiance in anyone. How dare you defy my orders. Leave the court at once and don't show me your face again," said King Krishna Dev Rai angrily.

"As you wish, My Lord!" saying this Tenali Ramakrishna left the court and went away.

The courtiers were feeling sorry for him. They were of the view that such a person, who is so witty and soft-spoken, should have a special place in the court. But they were helpless.

Next day when the court proceedings were in its full swing, and some serious discussion was going on, everyone's attention was suddenly drawn towards the main entrance of the court. A very strange kind of character was standing at the gate with an earthen pot on his head which had two holes. The person wearing it could see through those tiny holes.

"Who are you?" asked King Krishna Dev Rai.

"I am your court jester, My Lord," said Tenali Ramakrishna.

"But why have you covered your face with an earthen pot? And how dare you come back," said the King.

"My Lord! You never said that I should not come back. You only asked me not to show my face to you. And hence I have covered my face," said Tenali Ramakrishna.

The courtiers and the King had a hearty laugh.

King Krishna Dev Rai rose from his throne, embraced Tenali Ramakrishna in his arms, and said—

"Tenali Ramakrishna! I never meant to punish you. I only wanted to see the extent upto which you could apply your wits. I had ordered my guards secretly not to carry out the orders of execution. But so far as the instance of bribe is concerned, when you made your first entry, I took the right decision and the guard had to take all the fifty lashes." The King gave a momentary pause and then continued, "Tenali Ramakrishna! I am very much impressed by you. I appoint you my court jester from today. And I promise that you will never be subjected to any kind of punishment in future," saying this King Krishna Dev Rai gave his diamond studded necklace, in a symbolic gesture of affection, to him.

❏ ❏

3

SUBBA SHASTRI GETS A LESSON

There is a number of stories on the wits and intelligence of Tenali Ramakrishna. Each story tells us how cleverly he used to mould unfavourable circumstances into favourable ones. That too he used to do in such a manner that people would be roaring with laughter and yet none would be harmed. Sometimes he would create circumstances to teach someone a lesson also; but without meaning to be mean or harmful to that person. One thing about his acts was common that it used to be full of wisdom.

One such story is given below—

Once a horse trader from Persia came to Vijayanagar with some very good quality horses. King Krishna Dev Rai was known for his

25

fondness for horses. He had a very good collection of some very fine breeds of them. The King saw the horses that the horse trader of Persia had brought, and found them to be of a very high pedigree. He bought them all as he wanted his cavalry to be strengthened and properly equipped.

After the horse trader left, King Krishna Dev Rai gave one horse each to every soldier of his cavalry and asked them to take proper care of them, and train them suitably. The expenses on feeding and training of the horses was to be met from the royal treasure.

Tenali Ramakrishna approached the King and said that he too wanted a horse which he could train. The King gave him also a horse.

Tenali Ramakrishna brought the horse home and put it in a stable. But the strange thing that he did was, that he erected a wall and closed the entrance of the stable so that neither the horse could go out nor could anybody get in. Then he made a small opening in the wall in order to be able to cater to the horse's requirement of fodder.

Through that opening in the wall, Tenali Ramakrishna used to supply haystacks to the horse, which the horse would immediately grab in its month and pull inside. Water was also supplied through the same opening.

After about a month King Krishna Dev Rai wanted to know how the horses had grown; and how well they had been taken care of. All the soldiers of the cavalry brought their horses for King's inspection. The King was very happy to see that the horses had been taken full care of and they had grown beautifully. Suddenly the King noticed that Tenali Ramakrishna and his horse were not to be seen anywhere.

"Where is Tenali Ramakrishna," asked the King, looking around. "Tell him to come and see me with his horse."

A soldier went and informed Tenali Ramakrishna that the King wanted to see him along with his horse. But Tenali Ramakrishna came alone.

"Where is the horse? I am inspecting the horses today. I wanted to see how well they had been taken care of. Go and bring your horse also," said the King.

"Excuse me, My Lord! The horse you gave me turned out to be a bit to aggressive and stubborn. I wish I had brought it here, but it's not possible for me," said Tenali Ramakrishna.

"All right! In that case I am sending a few brave soldiers to bring the horse here," said the King.

"No, no, My Lord! Please don't do that. The horse had been taken care of by me—a Brahmin. So it would be better if you kindly send some Purohit with me to bring the horse here," said Tenali Ramakrishna with a mischievous smile.

There was a Purohit (a family priest) at the royal court of King Krishna Dev Rai, who used to perform sacerdotal functions of the royal family. His name was Subba Shastri.

The King immediately turned towards Subba Shastri who was standing nearby.

"Could you go with Tenali Ramakrishna and bring the horse from his stable," asked the King.

Subba Shastri, who was very jealous of Tenali Ramakrishna for his nearness to the King, didn't want to be let down. He said, "Of course I can bring that horse here. And what to talk of one horse, I can bring ten such horses, no matter how aggressive and stubborn they are."

"All right! In that case please come with me," said Tenali Ramakrishna.

"Subba Shastri Ji! You are a scholar. I am aware you have a deep study of Ashwashastra (the science of horses) also," said Tenali Ramakrishna to him when they reached home.

"Better late than never. At least now you have realised my greatness," said Subba Shastri combing his unusually long beard with his fingers.

"But, Shastri Ji! It's not an ordinary horse. I would like you to peep through the opening in the wall before you decide to demolish the rear wall of the stable and take out the horse," said Tenali Ramakrishna with a cunning smile on his face.

Tenali Ramakrishna had the right opportunity to settle his old scores with Subba Shastri that day.

But as soon as Subba Shastri inserted his head in the opening of the wall, the horse, taking his beard to be a haystack, grabbed it in his mouth. The horse was pulling his beard so hard that Subba Shastri's eyes welled up with tears and he began shrieking with pain.

Ultimately all the walls of the stable were demolished to get the horse out of the stable. But the horse was still holding his beard in his mouth. Having no alternative, they had to move towards the palace in that position only.

Now it had become clear to Subba Shastri that he had been pulling the legs of Tenali Ramakrishna every now and then and Tenali Ramakrishna had been looking for an opportune time to settle his scores with him.

When they reached the palace, the King and the soldiers of the cavalry were all waiting for them along with their horses. Seeing Subba Shastri in so funny a situation everyone roared with laughter. Even King Krishna Dev Rai was laughing uncontrollably. This made a difference. Hearing people laughing the horses too began neighing. The horse, which was holding the beard of Subba Shastri in his mouth, also began neighing. Subba Shastri's beard was freed as soon as the horse opened its month.

Suddenly the King became serious and stopped laughing. He said—

"Tenali Ramakrishna! I don't mind jests to create a humour. In fact it's healthy for everyone to laugh. But a laughter at the cost of someone's tears is surely unwelcome. What you have done to an honourable person like Subba Shastri is not advisable. This is disgraceful. I am sure you had this plan on your mind when you asked me for a horse. You must seek his apology."

But before Tenali Ramakrishna could seek an apology, Subba Shastri came forward and said—

"My Lord! It's not his fault. It's I Who should be blamed. I have always been pulling his legs, and at times I have also insulted him. But he has tolerated all my ill behaviour without saying a single word. And I did all this out of jealousy for him. What he has done to me was well deserved by me. In fact I have taken a lesson from what has happened today. He will be my mentor from today." Saying this Subba Shastri embraced Tenali Ramakrishna in his arms.

Tenali Ramakrishna also bowed before him and apologized for his deed.

King Krishna Dev Rai and the courtiers became very happy to see them becoming friendly with each other.

4

DEBATE OVER A RARE BOOK

King Krishna Dev Rai had many ministers at his court who were men of erudition and were very scholarly. Since the King himself was a great promoter of art, culture and literature, he used to hold debates on various topics among his Pundits.

But once a great Pundit from a neighbouring kingdom visited his court and challenged all the Pundits of his kingdom. He had a thorough knowledge of all the four Vedas and had indepth knowledge of various other branches. He had the reputation of defeating the greatest Pundits of every kingdom and had the honour of having been hououred by so many kings.

King Krishna Dev Rai was extremely worried to see that there was none in his kingdom to accept his challenge. He was happy that a great

scholar had come to his kingdom. He was of the view that having debate with such a man of erudition would enhance the knowledge of the scholars of his kingdom. Victory or defeat was secondary. But not being able to take the challenge would be simply shameful on their part.

However, King Krishna Dev Rai appointed a date for debate at his court. But nearer the date reached, the Asthana Pundit began becoming panicky. They were well aware of the fact that they could not match with the vast knowledge of the visiting Pundit. They thought that not being able to face the visiting Pundit would be shameful for them and the King as well; and facing the visiting Pundit and being defeated too would be just as shameful. Naturally, they decided to consult Tenali Ramakrishna as the last resort. They all went to his house and began pleading with him—

"O Tenali Ramakrishna! We have come to take refuge in your shelter. The visiting Pundit is a man of erudition. He is a great scholar. He has a thorough knowledge of all the four Vedas; and besides the

knowledge of the Vedas he has an indepth knowledge of various other branches of learning also. He has been honoured by so many kings of different kingdoms and has defeated so many Pundits in debate. We shall not be able to match his vast knowledge."

"What do you expect me to do? I am only a jester, not a scholar," said Tenali Ramakrishna scratching his temple.

"Oh, you can certainly do a lot. Wits work where wisdom and learning fail," said the Asthana Pundits.

Tenali Ramakrishna pondered the issue for a while, then he nodded and said—

"All right! This is going to be the biggest challenge of my life; but rest assured, I shall definitely do something and defeat the visiting Pundit. Now go back home and have a comfortable sleep. Leave the rest to me."

Being assured thus the Asthana Pundits became very happy and returned.

On the appointed date of debate the court was filled with courtiers and other dignitaries. King Krishna Dev Rai was also there but looked extremely worried. He was confident of Tenali Ramakrishna's capability of performing jests, but that he would be able to defeat a great scholar in debate was doubtful.

The visiting Pundit was given an appropriate seat and now everyone was eagerly waiting for Tenali Ramakrishna to come. But they didn't have to wait for long. Tenali Ramakrishna came in the guise of a Pundit. He had an extremely large size packet in his hands. The packet was wrapped in a red silk cloth and it gave an appearance of volumes of books.

Tenali Ramakrishna first bowed before the king and then prostrated himself before the Pundit.

"O scholar of scholars! Kindly accept my salutations in your honour before we enter into a debate," said Tenali Ramakrishna humbly.

King Krishna Dev Rai understood that Tenali Ramakrishna was on to something but he was not aware of what his jester had planned.

The King looked around and then announced—

"Now two great Pundits are sitting before each other. Everyone is waiting impatiently for the debate to begin. Let the debate begin."

Tenali Ramakrishna began—

"O great scholar! Though I have defeated many Pundits in debate, I am nothing before you. And it is for this reason that I have brought this rare book with me so that I may enter into debate with a man of erudition like you. Will you be kind enough to allow me to begin our debate on this rare book?"

The visiting Pundit did not know which book it was. So he asked—

"What is the name of this rare book, sir?"

"Oh, the name of this book is—'Thilakasta Mahisha Bandhana'," said Tenali Ramakrishna looking into his eyes.

The visiting Pundit became nervous as he was not aware that any such book existed on earth. He thought that if he entered into a debate with a scholar who had studied the book, which he had not even heard of, he was sure to be defeated. But his plight was that he could not admit that he had not even heard of that book. That would show his lack of knowledge. So exhibiting a great deal of confidence on his face he said—

"Oh, sir! You are talking of that rare book. I remember having read it during my childhood. But it's so long a period now that I have forgotten many chapters of it. I would like to go through the book again tonight and then we shall have a debate on the subject tomorrow."

"Oh sure, why not sir? You are our honourable guest and it's our moral duty to meet your requirements. We shall meet tomorrow, sir," said Tenali Ramakrishna exhibiting extra humbleness.

The visiting Pundit returned to the royal guest house. He was greatly worried. He was thinking that he wouldn't be able to study so big a book, which contains volumes and volumes of knowledge, in one night. The result would be a sure humiliation. He would have to forego all his titles if he lost in the debate. Worried thus the visiting Pundit collected all his disciples and fled the place in the middle of the night.

It came like a shock to King Krishna Dev Rai when he was informed that the visiting Pundit had fled along with his disciples in the middle of the night. He turned towards Tenali Ramakrishna and said, "What trick did you play on that poor Pundit? I am surprised that a great scholar like him had to leave our royal guest house stealthily because of you. And what was that rare book you said yesterday? O God! It was so voluminous a book."

Tenali Ramakrishna said, "My Lord! I called it 'Thilakasta Mahisha Bandhana'. But the fact is that no such book exists on earth.

"But you did have a voluminous book wrapped in a red silk cloth," said the King not being able to understand anything.

"My Lord!" said Tenali Ramakrishna with a mischievous smile, "It was no book at all. It was only a bundle of sticks which I had tied together with a rope, put it in a box, and wrapped around it a silk cloth to make it look like a voluminous book," and then giving a hearty laugh he said, "and that poor Pundit was claiming that he had read the book during his childhood."

Now everyone understood what Tenali Ramakrishna had actually done. The King and the courtiers had a hearty laugh. They were all full of praise for him.

"Tenali Ramakrishna! I am once again greatly impressed by you. Using your wits and applying your wisdom, you have saved us from sure humiliation. Your name will appear in golden letters in the history of Karnataka," saying this King Krishna Dev Rai embraced Tenali Ramakrishna and rewarded him suitably.

❏ ❏

5

THE LAST WISH OF THE KING'S MOTHER

Once King Krishna Dev Rai's mother fell seriously ill. Due to old age and physical infirmity she couldn't respond to best available medicines in the kingdom. While she was on her deathbed she wished to distribute mangoes among Brahmins. But she succumbed to death without her wish being fulfilled. The reason why her wish could not be fulfilled was that it was not the season for mangoes. The whole kingdom felt woebegone on the sad demise of King Krishna Dev Rai's mother.

The King was feeling extremely sad that his mother's last wish, which was so simple, could not be fulfilled. He was worried that her soul wouldn't rest in peace in the other world unless her last wish was fulfilled. So after performing the last rites of his mother, he summoned his Purohit and consulted him on this matter.

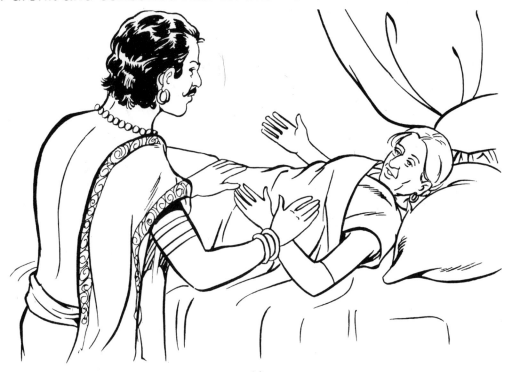

"Purohit Ji! My mother had a simple wish while she was on her deathbed. She wanted to distribute mangoes among Brahmins. Unfortunately it was not the season for mangoes, and I could not fulfil her last wish. Now I seek your advice. Please tell me what to do."

"My Lord!" said the Purohit sensing the plight of King Krishna Dev Rai, "It's something very serious. Last wish not being fulfilled keeps a soul wandering in the magnetic field of the earth only. The soul is liberated only after the fulfilment of the wish. Had she been alive, distribution of mango fruit would have solved the problem. But now since she is in her heavenly abode, distribution of simple mango fruit wouldn't serve the purpose. You will have to distribute mangoes, made of gold, among the Brahmins. And only then her soul will be liberated."

King Krishna Dev Rai readily agreed to it. On an auspicious day he distributed mangoes made of gold among the Brahmins, and was satisfied that he had done his solemn duty.

Tenali Ramakrishna was a witness to all this, and was very much irritated to see how the Purohit and the other Brahmins had fooled the King. He didn't say anything, but decided that he would teach them a lesson.

Tenali Ramakrishna, after a gap of a few days, approached the Purohit and the other Brahmins, and made a humble entreaty—

"Respected sirs! I was very impressed to see how you liberated the soul of our King's mother. Tomorrow is my mother's death anniversary. Can I expect you all to come to my house and perform certain rites on her death anniversary?"

The Purohit and the other Brahmins were very happy at this invitation. They thought—'Tenali Ramakrishna is a rich man. He has been handsomely rewarded by the King so many times. He will definitely give us a lot of remuneration for performing the rites.'

Thinking thus, the Purohit and the Brahmins gave their consent and promised to go to Tenali Ramakrishna's house the next day.

Next day when the Purohit and the Brahmins reached Tenali Ramakrishna's house, he was already waiting for them. He invited them in and closed the doors from all sides after making them sit comfortably.

"Please wait for some time; I am making certain preparations," saying this Tenali Ramakrishna placed some iron rods in the fire and began heating them.

The Purohit and the Brahmins were watching him intently. They found it very strange. They were expecting that Tenali Ramakrishna would offer them a sumptuous meal and a handsome remuneration. But there were no signs of any of these. After having waited for a long time the Purohit and the Brahmins lost their patience. One of them said—"Tenali Ramakrishna! We fail to understand your purpose. You invited us to perform rites on your mother's death anniversary. We are sitting idle and you are heating rods. This has no connection with the performance of rites."

"No, it does have connection," said Tenali Ramakrishna. "My mother suffered from arthritis when she was on her deathbed. She used to whine with pain. She used to ask me to heat an iron ord and place it on her body. And it really used to bring relief to her. One day, when she was in her last days, she got a severe attack of arthritis and asked me to heat an iron rod. I was heating the rod in the furnace, but before I could take the heated rod to her, she had already breathed her last. I feel so sorry that I couldn't fulfil her last wish. Her soul must be wandering in the magnetic field of the earth. It must be liberated. I am sure, putting the heated rod on the bodies of all of you will definitely cause relief to her, and her soul will be liberated."

The Purohit and the Brahmins became very nervous. They were almost scared to death.

At last the Purohit gathered some courage and said—

"Tenali Ramakrishna! You are an intelligent man. How do you expect to liberate your mother's soul by putting heated iron rods on our bodies? This theory has no basis."

"Why this theory has no basis?" said Tenali Ramakrishna a bit angrily, "If the soul of the King's mother could be liberated by you all by taking mangoes made of gold, why can't my mother's soul be liberated by taking heated iron rods on your backs? The King's mother's last wish was to distribute mangoes, and my mother's last wish was to take the heated iron rod on her back; this is the only difference. But the common thing among the two is the liberation of soul."

Hearing this the Purohit and the Brahmins became very nervous. They began pleading for mercy.

"Tenali Ramakrishna!" said to the Purohit, "It is clear to us now that you have brought us here to teach a lesson. We admit our fault. We are ready to give all the golden mangoes to you; we also promise that we shall never repeat this in future. Now do kindly excuse us and please don't put these heated iron rods on our backs."

"If indeed you are sorry for your deed, please go to the king and return the golden mangoes to him and apologize," said Tenali Ramakrishna.

King Krishna Dev Rai couldn't understand anything when the Purohit and the Brahmins reached the palace to return the golden mangoes. The Purohit explained everything to the King and apologized.

King Krishna Dev Rai immediately sent for Tenali Ramakrishna.

"Why did you do this," asked the King.

"My Lord! These Brahmins are your subjects. And your subjects are supposed to be loyal to you. Whereas they have cheated you. If they can afford to cheat their king, what would they be doing to ordinary people of your kingdom. What I have done was only with a purpose to teach them a lesson. I meant no harm to them. I only wanted to curb their practice."

King Krishna Dev Rai thought for a while and then said, "What Tenali Ramakrishna says is correct. I agree with him. Take the golden mangoes back. A king never takes back what he gives. But don't be greedy and don't cheat anyone in future; this is a warning."

Then Krishna Dev Rai rewarded Tenali Ramakrishna suitably for opening his eye.

❏ ❏

6

A LINGUIST

A linguist is a person who is accomplished in several languages. One day one such linguist arrived at the gate of the palace of King Krishna Dev Rai and began talking to the guards in Kannada language. There were some other guards from Andhra Pradesh and Tamil Nadu. He began talking to them in Telugu and Tamil languages. There were also some other guards with whom he talked in Marathi and Malyalam languages. But all that he conveyed in so many different languages was that he wanted to see King Krishna Dev Rai.

"Could you tell me why is it that you want to see the King," enquired the head of the guards.

And then without waiting for a reply from the stranger, the head of the guards discussed the matter with the other guards and allowed him to go in and see the King.

The stranger entered the court and bowed before King Krishna Dev Rai. After finishing his talk with his royal guest, who had come from some other country, the King turned toward the stranger and said, "You must be coming from a distant place. Tell me, why is it that you wanted to see me.

"My Lord! I am only a traveller," said the stranger, "I do not want any undue favour from you. I do not want any money either. I have come to pay a visit to your court. Your ministers are said to be the best brains in India. I would like to know if there is anyone at your court who can tell my mother-tongue."

"It's quite a challenge. Isn't it?" said King Krishna Dev Rai with a smile, "You must have mastered a number of languages I guess. I am happy to learn that you have no greed for reward or for anything. But at least you can accept our hospitality. You will be our royal guest. Get fresh, have your dinner. We shall discuss the matter tomorrow. I too will be glad to know the number of languages that you have accomplished."

Meanwhile a courtier began talking to him in Gujarati. The stranger smiled and answered him in Gujarati.

"He is a Gujarati, My Lord," said a courtier who was from Gujarat.

But the stranger smiled and said that he was not a Gujarati.

"He is a Marathi, My Lord," said one of the two soldiers with whom he had talked in Marathi.

But the stranger said that he was not Marathi either.

"He is from Kerala, My Lord," said a guard with whom he had talked in Malayali language. But the stranger denied that he ever belonged to Kerala.

"His mother-tongue is Tamil, My Lord," said an official with whom he had talked in Tamil. He is either from Madras or from Pondicherry. But he denied being a Tamil also.

Then a courtier began talking to him in Hindi. And when the stranger replied to him in perfect Hindi, the courtier declared him a person from Uttar Pradesh.

The stranger said, "I shall neither disclose my identity nor my mother-tongue. If I go on suggesting to you like that, you will ultimately know what my mother-tongue is. I might have told you lies in this respect. It wouldn't speak of your intelligence if you try all the languages on me. You may continue trying and I may continue denying. You can talk to me in Marathi, Bengali, Tamil, Gujarati, Telugu, Kannada, Malayalam, Kokni, Tulu Santhali or any other language spoken by the people of different regions in our country."

King Krishna Dev Rai began feeling uneasy sitting in his throne.

"Is there no one at my court who could take the challenge. I have got so many erudite scholars, so many learned ministers at my court, and there is none who can accept his challenge," said the King.

"I shall take the challenge," said Tenali Ramakrishna from a corner of the court, "but snice he must have travelled from quite a distance, he must be tired. My Lord! As already said by you I would also request him to get fresh, have a nice dinner and take rest in the night. Rest may be discussed tomorrow."

So the stranger was taken to the royal guest-house and was offered a nice dinner after he had had his bath. The stranger was happy that at least there was someone who accepted to take his challenge.

It was midnight. The stranger was sleeping peacefully on his cot. He had been served delicious meal at the dinner which he had eaten his fill. There was an oil lamp lit in that room. Suddenly a tall figure, covered from head to foot under a balnket, entered his room. The tall figure put out the lamp. It was a dark night with star-filled sky outside the window.

The mysterious figure tiptoed into the room, took out a matchstick from his pocket and inserted it lightly into the nostrils of the sleeping man. "Ha, ha, hachhoo!" The stranger suddenly woke up sneezing loudly. He saw a tall figure, covered under a balnket, in front of him.

"O Ma Kali! Save me from this ghost," yelled out the stranger in Bengali.

"So you are a Bengali," said the tall figure, "Please come in, My Lord. The mystery has been solved. He is a Bengali."

Then to his utter surprise, the stranger saw King Krishna Dev Rai, followed by other courtiers, ministers, and guards. And the man covered under blanket was none other than Tenali Ramakrishna who had accepted his challenge. They all looked happy and smiling.

"When someone is suddenly frightened by something, he speaks in his mother-tongue," said Tenali Ramakrishna To the stranger, "You prayed to your God in Bengali, and I am sure you are a Bengali."

The stranger bowed before King Krishna Dev Rai with respect and said—

"Now I can tell everyone that there is at least one person at your court who cannot be fooled. I happily accept my defeat.

❏ ❏

7

CHANGING A DOG'S COLOUR

The more Tenali Ramakrishna got close to King Krishna Dev Rai, the more some of the courtiers and ministers began getting jealous of him. The simple reason behind the mounting jealousy was that Tenali Ramakrishna was capable of making the King and others laugh and feel light with his jests, and with the result he was able to get special attention of the King, and often he used to be rewarded suitably.

Some of the courtiers and ministers hatched a plot to humiliate Tenali Ramakrishna.

One day, after having planned everything, they went to the royal barber and began praising him.

One courtier said, "Dear friend! Don't you realise that you are a royal barber and not an ordinary one? Every barber cannot go and give a shave and a haircut to the King. There definitely is something special in you that you are asked to attend on him. But still, you are not treated as honourably as Tenali Ramakrishna."

"Yes, just see, how unjust it is," said a minister, "Tenali Ramakrishna tells some stupid jokes to the King, and he is rewarded handsomely. What more does he do except performing some jests? Even if you become a court jester, we are sure, you will perform better than him."

The barber began feeling elated. He took a long breath, as if sighing, and said, "Sirs! You have put my feelings into your words. It's not that I have never noticed these things, but there is no way I can manage to achieve that high a status. Tell me, what I should do."

"Give a good shave to the King when you go tomorrow. And when you see him in good mood, tell him to replace Tanali Ramakrishna by you. Once you are appointed a court jester, you too will start getting handsome rewards and within no time you will become rich."

Next day the royal barber, after he had shaved off the beard of the King, seeing him in a pleasant mood, said, "My Lord! There is no other barber in your kingdom who could give you a better shave and haircut than I do. And our generations have been at your service in this job. The most unfortunate part of it is that I still am a barber. My coming generations will also remain barbers only. Whereas, there is no end to my plight when I see Tenali Ramakrishna flourishing and collecting handsome rewards for mere jests. Given a chance, I too can perform jests."

"What is it that you want exactly?" asked King Krishna Dev Rai with a smile.

"My Lord! I want to become a court jester at your court," said the royal barber haltingly, "and replace Tenali Ramakrishna."

King Krishna Dev Rai was startled to hear this. He contemplated the matter for some time and then agreed to appoint the royal barber as a court jester.

The proceedings began at the court and the royal barber took the seat of court jester. Tenali Ramakrishna appeared at the court at his usual time. He was terribly shocked to see the royal barber sitting in his seat. But he didn't say anything. He bowed before the king and left the palace. King Krishna Dev Rai also didn't say anything.

Tenali Ramakrishna began thinking of some way to counter the situation effectively. Suddenly a bright idea flashed across his mind when he saw a black stray dog passing by. He caught the dog, took it

to the heart of the town and began bathing and scrubbing it. People around were surprised to see this.

One passer-by stopped and asked, "Tenali Ramakrishna! I find it very strange. You hold a royal status at the court of the King; and a person of your status, bathing and scrubbing a dog in a public place, is simply beyond imagination. But I also understand, if you are doing it, there must be something special about it. Isn't it?"

"You have correctly understood," said Tenali Ramakrishna still scrubbing the dog vigorously, "I am changing the colour of this dog. I shall turn this dog from black to white by scrubbing it."

"What did you say? Have you gone mad, Tenali Ramakrishna? Is it possible to change the colour of someone's skin, or the colour of some animal's fur. Tenali Ramakrishna! Go and consult some doctor. There is something seriously wrong with you," said another passer-by.

"There isn't anything wrong with me. I am in perfect health. Would you please mind your business and let me do my job?" said Tenali Ramakrishna rather angrily.

After that none said anything to him and he continued bathing and scrubbing the dog. But the message spread like wildfire. Gradually the news reached the ears of King Krishna Dev Rai also. He smiled and was sure that Tenali Ramakrishna was upto something. He sent for him.

Meanwhile the royal barber had tried to perform all kinds of jests, told so many jokes, but had failed miserably in making the King and the courtiers laugh.

Suddenly Tenali Ramakrishna was seen coming to the court holding a black dog in his side still dripping wet. His mere presence sent the King and the courtiers roaring with laughter.

"What is this, Tenali Ramakrishna?" asked the King still laughing.

"This is a dog," was the short reply from Tenali Ramakrishna.

Again everyone roared with laughter.

"That is evidently true," said the King, "but what I have been informed is rather silly."

"And what is it that sounds so silly to you?" asked Tenali Ramakrishna.

The King said, "I have been informed that you are trying to change the colour of this dog. Isn't it sheer madness? Is it possible to change someone's colour?"

"I think it is, My Lord. Rather I would say anything is possible in your kingdom. If a barber can became a court jester, a black dog can also become white," saying this Tenali Ramakrishna bowed respectfully before the King and returned with the black dog.

This message also spread like wildfire and everyone came to know about this incident. And this became such a big problem for the royal barber that whenever he stepped out of his house people and young children would start calling him—'black dog', 'black dog'. With the result he stopped going out of his house.

When many days passed and the royal barber didn't show up, King Krishna Dev Rai sent for him. The royal barber came, but not to attend the court but to apologize.

"My Lord! I am extremely sorry. Kindly excuse me. I never wanted to become a court jester; it was only because of your ministers and courtiers that the greed for power, status and money got the better of me. I stopped going out of my house, because people have started calling me a 'black dog'. My Lord! I don't want anything. I will remain a barber only. Please call back Tenali Ramakrishna and reinstate him," said the royal barber with tears rolling down his cheeks.

"I am glad you understand," said King Krishna Dev Rai, "why Tenali Ramakrishna holds a special place here, and why he is so close to me. There are certain qualities in him which fetch him handsome rewards. And don't worry! I shall talk to the courtiers and ministers who led you to this shameful situation."

Tenali Ramkrishna was reinstated and the court was once again resounding with the laughters of the King, ministers and courtiers.

❏ ❏

8

WHOM DO BRAHMINS WORSHIP

Once court proceedings were going on at the court of King Krishna Dev Rai and since there wasn't anything serious to be disposd of, the King chose a topic of debate—

"Dear ministers and courtiers! Today we don't have anything serious to discuss and dispose of. By God's grace no problem has been put up before me. So let us select a topic of debate. Is there anyone among our able ministers and courtiers who would like to suggest a topic?"

"My Lord! We leave it to you to select the topic," said Tenali Ramakrishna.

King Krishna Dev Rai thought for some time and then said—

"As everyone of you is aware that Brahmins are revered by Vaishyas, Kshatriyas and Shudras; I would like to know if there is anyone who knows as to whom do the Brahmins revere."

The question seemed very simple to all the ministers and courtiers.

"It's very simple, My Lord. Brahmins revere cows, which are symbolic of Kamadhenu," said one of the ministers. And almost everyone agreed to it.

"What is your opinion, Tenali Ramakrishna? Do you agree with this answer?" asked the King.

"In my opinion, My Lord," said Tenali Ramakrishna, "cows are revered by all. Be it human beings or gods. This is not I who says this. This has been said by our great scholars."

"If that be so, why Brahmins wear shoes made of cowhide?" asked the King again.

What King Krishna Dev Rai said was practically true. Everybody was silent. No one had an appropriate answer to this question. The

King announced that he would give one thousand gold coins to the person who would give a suitable reply to the question.

Everyone wanted to get one thousand gold coins in reward, but none could give a satisfactory reply.

Seeing everyone silent Tenali Ramakrishna rose from his seat and said—

"My Lord! The feet of Brahmins are considered very sacred; as sacred as the holy places where people go on pilgrimages. So wearing shoes by Brahmins, made of cowhide, gives salvation to cows."

"A wrong is after all a wrong. Wearing shoes made of cowhide can never be considered right; be it Brahmins or non-Brahmins. But I am happy you have given a witty reply. Here is your reward," saying this King Krishna Dev Rai gave Tenali Ramakrishna one thousand gold coins.

❑❑

9

A BURNT CHILD DREADS THE FIRE

Once a Persian trader arrived in Vijayanagar with some very good quality cats. The cats were so special that he wanted to give them to King Krishna Dev Rai as a gift. He brought his cats to the palace and met the King. The queen and the King both liked the cats very much. Though the trader said that he wanted to give the cats to the royal couple as a gift, the queen insisted that he should be given one thousand gold coins; not as a price but as a reward.

Later the Queen gave one cat each to her maids along with a cow to feed the cats with milk in order to keep them healthy.

One cat was given to Tenali Ramakrishna also along with a cow. The Queen instructed everyone that since the cats are of a very special breed, they must be taken full care of.

After a gap of one month King Krishna Dev Rai wanted to know how the cats had grown. All the maids brought their cats to the palace. Tenali Ramakrishna also brought his cat. All the cats looked very healthy, but Tenali Ramakrishna's cat was healthiest of all.

The Queen and the King were utterly surprised to see that Tenali Ramakrishna's cat was in the best of her shape. The reason behind their surprise was that once the King had given a horse to Tenali Ramakrishna for rearing; but despite the financial support from the royal treasure for rearing the horse, he had almost starved it to death. And this time, despite no financial support from the royal treasure except a cow for feeding the cat with milk, his cat had outgrown the other cats.

The Queen and the King were very happy to see such beautiful and healthy cats purring and playing around.

A silver bowl each of milk was given to all the cats to drink. All the cats drank milk from the bowls, but to the utter surprise of the Queen and the King, Tenali Ramakrishna's cat didn't even sniff at it. Instead the cat ran into the lap of Tenali Ramakrishna and began purring affectionately.

"Tenali Ramakrishna!" said King Krishna Dev Rai, "I have every genuine reason to be bewildered at the behaviour of this cat. Animals are guided by their natural instincts. No matter how thoroughly assuaged a cat may be, but it will drink milk at the first available opportunity; whereas your cat has acted much against its natural instinct. Could you please explain to me the reason behind it?"

"I agree, My Lord," said Tenali Ramakrishna, "but the cat is not to be blamed. In fact there is a well-known saying that the cats close their eyes while drinking milk; and I wanted to rid this cat from this bad habit. On the very first day when I took the cat home, I put boiling hot milk in a bowl and placed it before this cat. As is natural with the cats, this cat also put its mouth in the bowl with its eyes closed and burnt itself. It is since then that she has not touched milk."

Hearing this the Queen and the King burst into laughter.

"But your cat is in a very good state of health. How is it? It has not been drinking milk either," said King Krishna Dev Rai.

"My Lord! I had a lot of mice in my house. They had been causing damage to our clothes and other household things. I made use of this cat. Everyone of us knows that cats love eating mice. My Lord! There is a saying—'a burnt child dreads the fire.' I only took advantage of the situation. It couldn't drink milk because it had burnt its mouth, but it had to eat something in order to assuage its hunger, and mice are the best alternative for any cat on earth. Thus, I managed to save cow's milk for my children, and also didn't let the cat starve. You can yourself see, My Lord, that the cat is in the best of its health."

The Queen and the King had a hearty laugh and decided to keep the cat in the palace. They also allowed Tenali Ramakrishna to retain the cow with himself as a gift from the royal couple.

❑ ❑

10

A TRUNK FULL OF ORNAMENTS

Once some robbers gathered in a forest and began discussing their next target.

"We haven't robbed any house during the last two months," said the chief of the robbers, "and we have been so unfortunate that not a single passer-by has passed through this forest during these two months. Whatever we had is also coming to a finish. If things continue thus a day might come when we may have to starve."

"Yes, chief! What you say is correct, but we have already robbed all the wealthy houses in this area. Now they have nothing left in their houses. And robbing a poor man's house will yield hardly anything. It's no use taking risk for nothing," said a robber.

Another robber said, "But, chief! There is one person who is very rich and we haven't robbed his house yet. I am sure we shall get a lot of money and ornaments from his house. Enough to keep us going for one full year."

"Who is it?" asked the chief of the robbers curiously.

"It is Tenali Ramakrishna," spoke the same robber, "He is a court jester and is very close to the King. Quite often he gets very handsome rewards for performing jests at the court. The King likes him very much."

The chief of the robbers jumped with happiness.

The robbers made their plans to rob the house of Tenali Ramakrishna around midnight when the whole village would be deep asleep.

The band of robbers reached the house of Tenali Ramakrishna and hiding behind the fence around his premises, began waiting for midnight.

Meanwhile Tenali Ramakrishna came out of his dining room to wash his hands after dinner. He happened to see one of the robbers hiding behind the fence. But he was not a person who would paunic

71

under such circumstances. Instead of getting nervous he began thinking of a plan to counter the situation.

He called his wife in a loud voice, loud enough to make the robbers hear—

"Dear! In the recent past there have been lots of cases of robbery in our village and also in the neighbouring villages. Our King also seems to be in no mood to take such happenings seriously. Look at his indifference towards such happenings; he has not even cared to deploy his soldiers in the villages which are so close to the forest. Now it is all on us either to safeguard our belongings ourselves or allow the robbers to take them away."

By then Tenali Ramakrishna's wife had also come out and joined him. But she was not able to understand anything. Tenali Ramakrishna continued, "Do one thing. Put all the money and your ornaments in the big trunk that is lying in the store room." Tenali Ramakrishna's wife opened her mouth to say something but he winked and raised a cautionary finger which was enough for her to grasp its meaning.

"Yes, you are absolutely right!" said she, "The King has given us so much; we cannot allow it to be taken away just like that. We shall put all our valuable belongings in the trunk and lock it."

"No, no, that will not be sufficient. It would be no problem for the robbers to break the lock, once they break into our house. The safest way to safeguard our belonging is to throw the trunk into this well. But, remember one thing—you will not disclose the matter to anyone in the village," saying this Tenali Ramakrishna and his wife went back into the house and began stuffing the trunk with heavy stones.

After some time the robbers saw Tenali Ramakrishna and his wife pulling a trunk with great difficulty. They somehow managed to drag the trunk to the well, and then applying all their energy they pushed the heavy trunk into the well.

The chief of the robbers became very happy. He said to the robbers in a whispering tone—

"See this fool has made our job so easy. He has saved us the trouble of breaking into his house and searching for valuables. All that we have to do now is to take the trunk out of the well after midnight when they are deep asleep."

All the robbers agreed with the plan. But Tenali Ramakrishna, stealthily managed to sneek through the back door and hid himself in a dark corner. Now he was waiting for the robbers to get into action.

He heard the chief of the robbers telling his friends—"Now it's time for us to get into action. First thing that we have to do is to drain out water from the well with the help of this rope and bucket. And when the well becomes dry it will become easy for us to get the trunk out."

All the robbers began drawing water from the well and pouring into the channel by the side of the well. The water began flowing through the channel into the field. Tenali Ramakrishna had made this channel to water the plants in his field. He was watching the whole thing quietly. Suddenly he thought—'Why not make use of their labour. They are drawing plenty of water.' And thinking this he immediately swung into action. He took a spade and began making way for water to flow to each and every plant in his field.

After all the plants had been watered and the robbers were still busy drawing water from the well, Tenali Ramakrishna made yet another plan. He quietly slipped from his field and set out to the palace hiding himself from the eyes of the robbers.

He informed the guards at the palace gate of the whole sequence of happenings. The guards went to barracks to wake up soldiers and send them with Tenali Ramakrishna.

Within moments Tenali Ramakrishna was going back to his house with a few chosen armed soldiers; all tiptoeing.

The robbers were still busy drawing water from the well without knowing that they had been fully surrounded by the royal soldiers. The armed soldiers suddenly launched an attack on the robbers, and seeing the number of soldiers, the robbers surrendered without much resistance.

Next day they were brought before King Krishna Dev Rai, and he ordered them to be hanged to death.

Tenali Ramakrishna was rewarded sumptuously for his valour and presence of mind.

❑ ❑

11

AN ASTROLOGER'S PROPHECY

King Krishna Dev Rai was a great lover of art, culture and literature, but at the same time he was matchless in wielding his sword also. He was a great warrior. The subjects of Karnataka were lucky, and they also acclaimed him widely to be the greatest warrior ever heard of.

Once a king of his neighbouring kingdom waged a war against him. King Krishna Dev Rai ordered his Army Generals to make necessary preparations in order to be able to counter his enemy suitably, and summoned the royal astrologer for consultation.

"Pundit Ji! You are a great astrologer! I have summoned you to consult your ephemeris, make your calculations, and after studying the

position of stars, find the auspicious day on which I should move with my army to the battle field. You must be aware that my neighbouring king has declared war against me. Please also tell me the outcome of the war," said King Krishna Dev Rai to the astrologer.

The royal astrologer studied the stars, made calculations for hours, and then declared Tuesday as the most auspicious and suitable day for launching a counter attack. He said—

"My Lord! It is Tuesday when all the stars will be in favour of you, and you will be able to crush your enemy with all your might. A warrior like you, who commands his sword, rather whose sword always waits to obey the minutest gestures of the king of Vijayanagar, is sure to return victorious. Proceed with your army on Tuesday. Your sword is thirsty; quench its thirst with the blood of your enemy and add one more victory to the list of your glorious victories. You have the blessings of goddess Kali."

Tenali Ramakrishna was also present at the court when the royal astrologer was making prophecy and saying soothing words. Somehow he was not of the view that a king should depend solely on astrologers while taking such vital decisions. But he didn't say anything. He remained a silent spectator throughout.

Suddenly King Krishna Dev Rai turned towards Tenali Ramakrishna and said—

"What is your opinion, Tenali Ramakrishna? Should I act on the advice of the royal astrologer and make a move on Tuesday? What in your opinion will be the fate of the war?"

Tenali Ramakrishna thought for a while and then said, "My Lord! I have never been to a battlefield, and I have never witnessed a war. And I feel, giving opinion without having knowledge of something is very unwise. I have all along been a court jester only. I have never had exposure to any other field of life."

"In that case," said King Krishna Dev Rai, "I would suggest to you to accompany me to the battlefield. There you will have everything before your eyes, and will be able to benefit me with your valuable advices. Will this suit you?"

"There could not be a greater honour conferred on me by you, My Lord. I shall consider myself very fortunate to accompany you to the battlefield. At least I shall have a chance to make my King feel light in the evenings when he is tired after the whole day's battle. It is only then that my jests will get the real meaning. I thank you, My Lord, for this kind offer."

On Tuesday, after having had full preparations made, King Krishna Dev Rai proceeded with the army to the battlefield. He took Tenali Ramakrishna also with him.

Some of the courtiers and ministers, who were jealous of Tenali Ramakrishna, became very happy to see him going to the battlefield.

They were of the opinion that he could wield his pen only and not a sword; and was sure to be killed in the battlefield. And his death would bring an end to their hurdles.

When the army reached the battlefield, Tenali Ramakrishna, along with the King, observed the enemy's army minutely and said to King Krishna Dev Rai—

"My Lord! Your enemy has come with a big army. He has a lot of soldiers and also a lot of elephants in his army. Whereas the number of elephants in your army is less comparatively, but your elephants are quick and agile, and his elephants are fat and lazy. The number of horses in your army is far greater than the number of horses in his army. Your soldiers have been subjected to rigorous exercises, whereas his soldiers are fat and less trimmed which will definitely restrict their physical movement during combat. Moreover, the most important of all is that you have equipped your fighters with small size bows, whereas your enemies' fighters are equipped with large size bows. The large size bows will enable your enemy to launch an attack and shower arrows on your army from quite a distance, and that's precisely the reason why your enemy has formed an eagle maze to attack your army, My Lord. And for this kind of formation the appropriate antidote would be a crescent maze in which you will have to place two very strong and brave Generals of your army at each tip of the crescent. This kind of formation will close from both sides in a pincer movement and annihilate the army of your enemies. You are sure to gain victory, My Lord."

King Krishna Dev Rai was looking at Tenali Ramakrishna wide-eyed. He could not believe his ears. "Is it Tenali Ramakrishna, a court jester, or a warrior," thought the King.

"I terribly am at a loss of speech to see you speaking thus. I thought that you were merely a court jester and had no knowledge of things like

battle and war strategy. But I am simply overwhelmed to see you having thorough knowledge of war strategies also," said King Krishna Dev Rai.

"My Lord! Let me make a humble confession—it was not I but goddess Kali speaking through me. I indeed have no knowledge of war strategies," said Tenali Ramakrishna with folded hands.

"Tenali Ramakrishna!" said King Krishna Dev Rai in a choked voice, "I consider myself very fortunate to have brought you to the battlefield. I have already begun to feel that it is not I but goddess Kali who is leading this army; and so long as she is leading my army, there is no power on earth which can defeat my army," saying this King Krishna Dev Rai embraced Tenali Ramakrishna in the battlefield itself.

King Krishna Dev Rai and his army fought bravely and defeated the enemy badly. The enemy King succumbed to his injuries in the battlefield itself, and King Krishna Dev Rai returned victorious.

This particular war taught King Krishna Dev Rai to be more practical. He was so happy that he gave away the most handsome reward to Tenali Ramakrishna he had ever received in his life.

❏ ❏

12

A CHILD IS ABOVE A KING

After winning the great war and crushing his enemy for ever, King Krishna Dev Rai had become an egotist, and possessed a most colossal ego that shaded his real personality and marred his popularity among his subjects.

Everyone was surprised to see the sudden change in him. Tenali Ramakrishna too had noticed the change. He was worried and was thinking of putting him on the right track, and was waiting for the right opportunity.

One day he did get an opportunity when King Krishna Dev Rai called him and said—

"Tenali Ramakrishna! Do you notice that all the kings are afraid of me. They have begun sending presents to me. What they send is not important; the most important thing is that this is their symbolic gesture of accepting my superiority over them. Ramakrishna! Don't you think that I am the greatest of all? Does anyone possess so many qualities at a time? See, I am an art lover, I do everything to promote culture and literature, I am a great warrior, I have managed to keep my administration in perfect order, I am more popular among my subjects than any other king on earth. All these qualities combined together make a great personality; and it is only I who possesses so many qualities at a time. There is no one greater than me," King Krishna Dev Rai would have continued his soliloquy had he not been interrupted by Tenali Ramakrishna.

"My Lord! There is none who does not admire your greatness. But please don't get carried away. You are not the greatest one," said Tenali Ramakrishna in a humble voice.

"What nonsense? How dare you say that? Ramakrishna! You will have to prove your point, or else you will be beheaded," said the King angrily.

"My Lord! A child is greater than you," said Tenali Ramakrishna humbly.

"All right! I give you one week's time. That's all! You may go now," King Krishna Dev Rai was terribly angry with him.

Tenali Ramakrishna left the court immediately and went home. It was precisely after three days that he happened to see a very beautiful child. He picked up the child, took permission from the parents of the child and went straight to the palace. When he reached there, King Krishna Dev Rai was with the Queen in his Antahpura; and being in Antahpura meant that only a select few could visit the King. Tenali Ramakrishna reached the Antahpure with the child, where King Krishna Dev Rai was busy talking to the Queen.

The Queen became very happy to see the beautiful child and immediately took it in her lap. She began fondling and kissing the child, and the child also began trying to feel her nose-ring with its chubby little fingers. The child made her cheeks and nose wet with its saliva; and the Queen seemed to be thoroughly enjoying it. But Tenali Ramakrishna was terribly shocked to see the child making the Queen's valuable clothes wet. And the most surprising thing was that the Queen didn't at all mind it.

After some time King Krishna Dev Rai also took the child in his arms and began tossing it in air. The innocent child began making funny sounds joyfully and then, suddenly, it caught the moustache of the King with its little fingers. Tenali Ramakrishna immediately, rushed forward, but King Krishna Dev Rai stopped him, saying—"Ramakrishna! Let him play with me. Don't disturb him. A child is like God. He can do anything."

This was the oportune time for Tenali Ramakrishna. He said, "My Lord! I have proven my point."

King Krishna Dev Rai Turned towards him and asked— "What point?"

"My Lord! Just now you have said that a child is like God. And I am sure you are aware that God is greater than you. My Lord! You became angry with me when I said that a child is greater than you, and you said that you would have me beheaded if I didn't prove my point. But by goddess Kali's grace you yourself have proven my point," said Tenali Ramakrishna.

"I must admit that you have applied the most subtle method to prove your point and also bring me back to the right track," saying this King Krishna Dev Rai rewarded Tenali Ramakrishna suitably. And the Queen gave a lot of ornaments, toys, and one thousand gold coins to the child before Tenali Ramakrishna could take the child back to its parents.

13

A BOUT WITH A WRESTLER

Wits work where might doesn't.

Often King Krishna Dev Rai would be in a situation when a challenge would be thrown and there would be no one in his kingdom to counter the might of the challenger. It is under such circumstances that, Tenali Ramakrishna would apply his wits and wisdom and get King Krishna Dev Rai out of the humiliating situation.

One such situation arose when a great wrestler from the Punjab visited his kingdom and threw a challenge. He was a giant of a man. The general height of the people of Karnataka was not even upto his shoulders. He had a big chest, extremely powerful arms, pillar-like

thighs, and the biceps in his upper arms were almost as big as the waist of an average person in the kingdom of King Krishna Dev Rai. The sound of his footsteps could be heard from quite a distance when he would be walking in the streets.

King Krishna Dev Rai summoned all the great wrestlers of his kingdom and asked if there was anyone who was ready to take the challenge of the giant of the Punjab.

The all-time champion of wrestling of his kingdom, who had won a lot of medals in and outside Karnataka, came forward and said—

"My Lord! We are wrestlers and have defeated many great wrestlers in wrestling bouts. We are not cowardly. We can accept a challenge from any wrestler, but the wrestler has to be a human being; not a giant like him. The wrestler, who has come from the Punjab, is so big and tall that we are no match to him. Our hands won't even reach his neck, if he stands straight, which is an essential part of the beginning of a wrestling bout. My Lord! Accepting the challenge would bring us sure defeat, which will be very humiliating for us and for you as well."

"I understand your point," said King Krishna Dev Rai worriedly, "but I cannot allow him to return just like that. Just imagine! He will leave this kingdom, go to some other kingdom and will tell everyone there that there was none in Karnataka who could take my challenge. That will bring us a very bad name and would be worse than a defeat in a wrestling bout. No, no, do something; I won't allow this to happen."

The wrestlers returned grim-faced debating the impossible situation.

"I have heard a lot about Tenali Ramakrishna, who is a court jester at the court of the King," said one of the wrestlers, "It is said that he has the blessings of goddess Kali and is capable of solving very complicated issues."

"Come on! Don't be silly! He is a man of frail personality. He may be good at performing jests; he may be good at composing meaningful poems, but you would be considered silly if you expect him to wrestle with the giant," said the other wrestler, and spoke yet another one—

"If you send him into the arena to wrestle with the giant of the Punjab, you shall have to keep yourself prepared with a bier outside the arena."

All the wrestlers began laughing at this aukward joke.

"You couldn't quite get what I meant," said the first wrestler, "See, there is a saying—'Wits work where might doesn't'—and it is on that basis that I am suggesting to you all to consult that wise man. He may be able to find some way out."

"You are probably right," agreed all the other wrestlers.

Talking thus, they went to the house of Tenali Ramakrishna.

"Sir," said the champion, "we are wrestlers."

"Yes, that's apparent," said Tenali Ramakrishna, "What is it that you want? Please tell me your purpose."

"Sir, we are facing a great problem. We don't know how to tackle the situation. In fact a great wrestler from the Punjab has come and thrown a challenge. The problem is that he is too big in size and is strong like steel. Our King says that someone of us has to take his challenge; he should not be allowed to go away just like that. But the problem with us is that if we take the challenge, we are sure to face defeat. And the defeat will not bring humiliation to us only, it will bring humiliation to our King as well. But letting him go without accepting his challenge would be even more humiliating," said the champion of the wrestlers.

Tenali Ramakrishna listened to them patiently and realised the grimness of the situation. He contemplated the issue for sometime and then said—

"Look, brothers! It's a difficult situation. We have no alternative but to accept his challenge. It will need more of our brain power than that of our physical power." Tenali Ramakrishna paused for a moment and

then continued, "In fact, due to certain unavoidable reasons, I could not attend the court today, or else, I would have known about it. But anyway...don't worry. Go and tell the King that Tenali Ramakrishna has accepted the challenge of the great wrestler of the Punjab. The King may fix up a suitable day for the bout."

"But, sir! How will you manage to wrestle with him? It's probably because you haven't seen him that you are talking thus," said the wrestler.

"Oh, leave that to me. It's my headache now," Tenali Ramakrishna assured them.

King Krishna Dev Rai became very happy to learn that Tenali Ramakrishna had accepted the challenge. The King knew that his court jester must have hit upon some novel idea to counter the challenge of the giant. Fully assured of the wits and wisdom of Tenali Ramakrishna, which inspired much confidence in him, he fixed up and announced a day next week for the much awaited bout. There was a wave of happiness throughout the kingdom.

On the appointed day for the bout, Tenali Ramakrishna was brought to the arena. As was planned, the great wrestlers of Karnataka had brought him on their shoulders, shouting slogans and cheering him. They had draped all their medals around his neck and were shouting— 'Guru Tenali Ramakrishna Zindabad' (long live Guru Tenali Ramakrishna).

The wrestler from the Punjab was totally confused to see a frail-looking man wearing so many medals. "It seems he is a great wrestler," thought he to himself.

Tenali Ramakrishna entered the arena, shook hands with the wrestler, and said, "O great wrestler! I am sure you must have gone through the 'Great Book of Wrestling' which tells about certain gestures the wrestlers are supposed to make and understand before the beginning of any bout. Your Guru must have taught you as I have taught these young wrestlers. Your Guru must also have taught you that there

are certain vital points in the body, which, if merely touched, will paralyse the lower limb of a person. Anyway...all that you have to do, before we start the bout, is to interpret the gestures made by me. If you interpret my gestures successfully, I shall believe that you are a real wrestler, and shall have a bout with you; but if you fail to interpret my gestures and still insist to have a bout with me, I shall touch the vital points in your body during the bout and paralyse your lower limbs permanently."

The wrestler from the Punjab was greatly confused. He had never been through this kind of situation all his life. Without being able to assess the seriousness of the situation, he agreed to interpret the gestures of Tenali Ramakrishna, thinking that if he succeeded in interpreting his gestures correctly, there was no harm in having a bout with the frail-looking wrestler; and if he could not, he would leave the arena instead of having a bout with him and getting his lower limbs paralysed permanently.

"Sir, I agree. Please show me the gestures," said the wrestler.

Then Tenali Ramakrishna began his gestures by stretching his right leg forward and touching the chest of the wrestler with his index finger. Then he touched himself with his left hand and again pressed his left hand with his right hand with great force. The wrestler kept looking at him like a fool, not being able to understand his gestures.

But this was not the end of his gestures. It seemed Tenali Ramakrishna wanted to confuse him completely. He again started making gestures. He pointed his right index finger towards south, and then joined his right and left index fingers to make a knot. He freed his index fingers, bent, and took a handful of sand from the ground and pretended to pour it into his mouth. Then he said—

"O wrestler! You have seen the gestures passed on from generation to generation. This is a code which must be known to all the wrestlers. Now its your turn. Please interpret the gestures made by me."

But the wrestler had not been able to interpret any of the gestures made by Tenali Ramakrishna. And as already agreed upon, he bowed before him and left the arena without having any bout. He was considering himself lucky that he had been able to save himself from getting paralysed permanently. But he was very angry that his Guru never told him anything about gestures which, according to Tenali Ramakrishna, was compulsory to have the knowledge of.

The Queen, the King and the spectators were simply awestruck to witness this kind of happening which was beyond their expectation and imagination.

"How could you manage this kind of miracle, Tenali Ramakrishna?" asked the King curiously, "I was thinking that the giant will crush you; but what we saw from a distance was that he bowed before you and left the arena. Tell me! I am dying of curiosity."

"Not only did he leave the arena without a bout, he gave all his medals also to me," said Tenali Ramakrishna.

King Krishna Dev Rai said with a smile, "But how did you manage this, you little devil?"

"My Lord! I only made a fool of him," saying this Tenali Ramakrishna narrated the whole sequence of happenings to the King.

The Queen and the King had a hearty laugh. The King asked, "And what did your gestures mean?"

"My Lord!" said Tenali Ramakrishna, "I meant by my gestures that the wrestler was strong and powerful like a right hand, and I was weak

like a left hand. If a wrestler, with a steel-like body would wrestle with so weak a person, the weak person would crack like a nut. And my next gesture meant that my wife is sitting among the spectators and has also come to see the bout. She is in the southern part of the pavilion. If you break my neck, she will become a widow, and shall have to eat sand."

"That was all I conveyed through my gestures to him, My Lord," said Tenali Ramakrishna with a furtive smile and lowered his head, trying to hide his countenance.

King Krishna Dev Rai roared with laughter. He rose from his place and embraced Tenali Ramakrishna affectionately. The Queen and the King were so happy with him that they immediately announced a handsome reward of one hundred thousand gold coins in favour of him.

❑ ❑

14

RESPECTABLE DONKEYS

Tenali Ramakrishna, apart from his matchless capability of performing jests, had a charismatic personality also. He was loved by all, excepting a very few who were jealous of him due to certain personal reasons.

One among the jealous ones was the family priest of King Krishna Dev Rai who used to perform all the sacerdotal rites of the royal family. The name of the family priest was Appalacharya. He was a Vaishnava and Tenali Ramakrishna was a Samartha Brahmin. These two sects never liked each other. Appalacharya used to think that since he was a family priest of a royal family and his sect was considered above the

Samartha Brahmin sect, he should be more close to the King; but the affection of King Krishna Dev Rai for Tenali Ramakrishna was not hidden from his eyes. And this pricisely was the reason why Appalacharya was extremely jealous of him.

Appalacharya would always try to let him down at the opportune time. Tenali Ramakrishna was aware of this fact, and always managed to corner him, using his wits and wisdom.

One fine morning, Tenali Ramakrishna went to the house of Appalacharya. He wanted to consult him and take his advice. Appalacharya saw him coming from a distance. Thinking that that was the right time to settle his score with him, he covered his face with a towel. Tenali Ramakrishna noticed it but didn't say anything.

"Good morning, Pundit Ji," said Tenali Ramakrishna with folded hands.

"Why, Tenali Ramakrishna? Why did you have to bring your inauspicious presence before me so early in the morning?" said Appalacharya curtly.

Tenali Ramakrishna was terribly hurt; but hiding his hurt feelings he said, "Pundit Ji! I came here to discuss something very important with you. But you don't seem to be in a good mood. Doesn't matter. We can leave it for some other day. Would you be kind enough to allow me to ask you a question?"

"You may ask, but be quick; I have got so many other important things to do," once again Appalacharya became curt.

"Don't worry, Pundit Ji! I won't waste your precious time. But may I ask you as to why you covered your face with your towel when you saw me coming?" asked Tenali Ramakrishna.

Now there was a cunning smile on the face of Appalacharya. He said, "Why? You are considered a man of wisdom throughout the kingdom, and you are not able to understand so simple a thing."

"Believe me, Pundit Ji! I have not been able to understand. Please explain to me," said Tenali Ramakrishna.

"Tenali Ramakrishna! You are aware that I am a Vaishnawa Brahmin and you a Samartha Brahmin. It is said that if a Vaishnava Brahmin sees a Samartha Brahmin early in the morning, the Vaishnava Brahmin is sure to be born as a donkey in his next birth. Now you yourself tell me who would like to be born as a donkey. This is the reason why I covered my face with my towel when I saw you coming from a distance. I wanted to avoid seeing your face early in the morning."

"What you say is correct, Pundit Ji. In future I shall try to avoid showing my face to you in the early morning. Good day! See you again," saying this Tenali Ramakrishna took leave of him and returned home.

Tenali Ramakrishna was thinking—'A man of erudition like Appalacharya is not expected to behave in such a foolish and rude manner. Why is it that he always tries to insult me? He must be taught a lesson.' And he began waiting for an opportune time.

Tenali Ramakrishna did get an opportunity when King Krishna Dev Rai, Appalacharya, and he himself, all were taking a morning walk and enjoying fresh air. There were a few donkeys grazing nearby. A bright idea flashed across his mind. He went straight to those donkeys and began bowing before them. The King and Appalacharya were greatly surprised to see him behaving thus. They also noticed him muttering something in an inaudible sound.

"Pundit Ji! Haven't you noticed that Tenali Ramakrishna has been behaving in a very stupid manner during the past few months," said the King.

"My Lord! You have only translated my feelings into your words. You are very correct. I too have been noticing the same. Just see, My Lord! What fun is it bowing before donkeys?" said Appalacharya in disgust.

But King Krishna Dev Rai had also an inkling that Tenali Ramakrishna was upto some mischief. It wasn't without purpose that he was bowing before donkeys. Hiding his smile, the King called him and said—

"Hey, Tenali Ramakrishna! What the hell are you doing? Do you think bowing your head before donkeys will lead you to greater wisdom?"

"My Lord!" said Tenali Ramakrishna, "It's not that I am bowing my head before these donkeys for no reason. In fact these donkeys are very respectable and must be revered by all. They were actually Vaishnawa Brahmins in their previous births. They are, in fact, kiths and kins of Pundit Appalacharya."

"What nonsense!" said the King angrily. "This is height of arrogance. Tenali Ramakrishna! You must know that performing jests is different from being arrogant. You have insulted an elderly person. You must apologize."

"But, My Lord! I have not insulted him. All the donkeys are the relatives of Pundit Appalacharya. And it is for this reason that I have paid respect to them," said Tenali Ramakrishna with folded hands.

"How do you relate Pundit Ji to these stupid donkeys?" asked the King still angry.

"My Lord! Pundit Appalacharya, one day, saw me early in the morning and covered his face with his towel. When I asked him the reason behind his funny behaviour, he said that if a Vaiahnava Brahmin sees a Samartha Brahmin early in the morning, he is sure to be born a donkey in his next birth. So thinking that these donkeys must have been Vaishnava Brahmins in their previous births, and must have seen some Samartha Brahmins early in the morning and as a result they may have taken birth as donkeys, I was bowing my head before them. In fact I have every genuine reason to pay my respects to them," Said Tenali Ramakrishna with a cunning smile on his face.

Pundit Ji immediately realised that he had once again been cornered by Tenali Ramakrishna.

King Krishna Dev Rai became very serious. He looked at Appalacharya and said—

"Pundit Ji! Scholars like you are supposed to have a broader perspective of life; people like you should be broad minded, or else, there would be no difference between you and an ordinary person," and then turning towards Tenali Ramakrishna, he added, "And Tenali Ramakrishna! What you have done today is definitely an eye-opener; but still, this was a crude method adopted by you.

Tenali Ramakrishna and Appalacharya, both embraced each other and vowed to forget their differences.

❑ ❑

15

SMOKE OF THE LENGTH OF TWO ARMS

Funny title of a story! Isn't it? But this is how things were during those old days. Kings used to pose difficult problems, sometimes almost impossible ones, before their ministers and courtiers and ask for solutions. And then someone would come out with a solution to an impossible-looking thing, and would be sumptuously rewarded.

One day some light discussion was going on at the court between the King and the courtiers, when suddenly a topic was broached on intelligence. Most of the ministers and even the spiritual preceptor of the King were jealous of Tenali Ramakrishna. This turned out to be an opportune time for them to put up their argument before the King. So one minister said, "My Lord! There is no dearth of intelligent ones at your court, and if given a chance it can be proved, but...."

"But, what minister?" asked the King curiously.

"I shall tell you, My Lord," said the commander-in-chief rising from his seat, "The minister wants to say that no one gets a chance to prove his intelligence in the presence of Tenali Ramakrishna. Everytime he foils our attempts to prove our wisdom and takes the credit himself. My Lord! Just think! how is it possible for us to prove our capability, unless we are given a chance?"

"So, that's the matter," King Krishna Dev Rai became serious. It had become clear to him that all the courtiers were aganist Tenali Ramakrishna. He kept thinking for some time. Suddenly his eyes were fixed on a lighted incense in front of the statue of Lord Vishnu. He immediately thought of a plan to test the courtiers. He said, "All of you will definitely be given a chance to prove your capability. Tenali Ramakrishna will not be allowed to come in your way."

All the courtiers became very happy.

"What shall we have to do, My Lord, to prove our capability?" said one of the courtiers.

"All of you must be seeing the smoke rising from the lighted incense. Bring me the smoke from the lighted incense of the length of two arms," the King signalled to the lighted incense and said, "One who succeeds in performing this job, will be considered cleverer than Tenali Ramakrishna."

All the courtiers were taken aback to see the King posing such a problem before them. "How foolish is it to test our capability in this manner?" thought the courtiers. "How is it possible to measure a thing like smoke?" But the courtiers had to find some way. Many courtiers tried to measure the smoke coming out of the lighted incense, but all in

vain. The smoke would rise above and wave in a snaky movement. They kept trying from morning till evening, but neither it was possible for them, nor could they do it.

King Krishna Dev Rai was smiling furtively. After all the courtiers were tired of it, one of the courtiers said, "My Lord! As far as a think, it is impossible to measure smoke. If Tenali Ramakrishna succeeds in doing it we shall accept him as cleverer than all of us. But if he too fails to do it, he should be considered on a par with us, and should not be given more importance.

King Krishna Dev Rai looked at Tenali Ramakrishna with a smile and said, "Do you accept this challenge?"

"I can only try, My Lord," said Tenali Ramakrishna, rising from his seat and bowing humbly before the King, "As always, I shall obey your orders this time also."

Tenali Ramakrishna motioned to a servant and whispered something in his ear. The servant immediately went away. There was complete silence at the court. Everyone was curious to see how Tenali Ramakrishna measures the smoke rising from the lighted incense and gives a length of two arms of it to the King. Just then the servant appeared at the court with a glass tube in his hands, sealed on top and open at the bottom, and was of a length of two arms. Tenali Ramakrishna took the glass tube to the lighted incense and positioned it above the rising smoke, keeping the mouth of the tube facing it. The smoke started filling the tube, and within no time the tube was completely filled

112

with smoke. Tenali Ramakrishna stuffed a piece of cloth in the mouth of the glass tube to stop the smoke from coming out of it.

Then handing it over to the King, he said, "My Lord! You wanted smoke of the length of two arms. This is it."

King Krishna Dev Rai took the glass tube filled with smoke, and wearing a smile on his face he turned towards the courtiers. All were sitting with their heads down. There were some who were not jealous of Tenali Ramakrishna. They were full of praise for him.

King Krishna Dev Rai said, "You people should accept at least now that Tenali Ramakrishna is intelligent and beyond comparison.

The courtiers had no reply.

❏ ❏

16

THE GREATEST GIFT

Once a neighbouring king attacked Vijayanagar.

Using his wits and military power, King Krishna Dev Rai won the battle and declared a victory celebration.

Due to certain unavoidable reasons, Tenali Ramakrishna somehow couldn't manage to come to attend the celebration at the right time.

After the celebration was over, King Krishna Dev Rai said, "This is not my victory alone; it's your victory as well. I have arranged to offer gifts to the courtiers on this occasion. All the members of the court may take the gifts of their choice.

On a dais were kept a lot of valuable gifts.

All the courtiers, including the prime minister, rushed at the dais and began picking up gifts of their choice, pushing each other.

The number of gifts was according to the number of courtiers.

In the twinkling of an eye, there was nothing left on the dais, except a silver dish.

Meanwhile, Tenali Ramakrishna arrived at the court. All the courtiers wore a furtive smile, thinking that he had come at a time when there was nothing left for him.

When Tenali Ramakrishna reached near the King, the King explained to him everything and said, "Your share of the gift, which is the only remaining item, is lying at the dais. You may please go and have it."

Tenali Ramakrishna went to the dais and picked up the silver dish with great respect and covered it with a piece of cloth.

All the courtiers were happy that Tenali Ramakrishna could get only a silver dish as gift in his share, whereas they had received valuable gifts.

King Krishna Dev Rai was greatly surprised to see Tenali Ramakrishna covering the empty silver dish with a piece of cloth in this manner. He asked with surprise—

"Tenali Ramakrishna! Could you explain to me why you covered the empty silver dish with a piece of cloth?"

"I did this in order to save your prestige, My Lord."

"I couldn't quite get it. How does this act of yours save my prestige?" asked the King.

"My Lord!" said Tenali Ramakrishna, "Till now, I have always received dishes full of gold coins and pearls from you. Just think, what impression will your subjects gather to see me carrying an empty silver dish from your palace? Will they not think, My Lord, that their King has got nothing left in his treasure, and that's the reason why he has given only an empty silver dish to Tenali Ramakrishna in gift."

"Oh", said the King and became very happy to see the shrewdness of Tenali Ramakrishna, "No, Tenali Ramakrishna! I won't give you an empty dish, not even today. Please uncover your dish," saying this King Krishna Dev Rai took out his valuable string of beads and put it in the empty silver dish.

This was the most expensive gift which Tenali Ramakrishna managed to get using his wits and presence of mind.

It was once again that Tenali Ramakrishna had managed to corner the jealous courtiers.

❑ ❑

17

REWARDING THE RIGHT PERSON

King Krishna Dev Rai had a hobby of collecting strange and rare things. And so the courtiers also used to be on the lookout for rare things that could fetch them handsome rewards. At times, some courtiers, given a chance, would also cheat them.

One day, one such courtier played a strange trick. He had brought a live peacock with red feathers. He said, "My Lord! I have taken great pains to get a strange peacock for you from the forests of Mysore."

Seeing the peacock with red feathers the King was greatly astonished. He thought to himself—'What great miracles the Nature performs. It's indeed the strangest peacock, I have ever seen." He immediately ordered that the peacock be kept in the royal garden and then he asked the courtier as to how much he had to spend in getting such a strange and rare peacock from out of the forests of Mysore.

"Thirty thousand in all," said the courtier.

King Krishna Dev Rai ordered an immediate payment of thirty thousand gold coins from his royal treasure. He also assured the courtier that he would be suitably rewarded for having managed the rarest thing on earth.

What more could the courtier have wanted. Getting thirty thousand gold coins was no less a reward for him. He had applied a little brain and spent some one hundred gold coins in arranging this kind of peacock for the King.

Tenali Ramakrishna too saw the peacock, but somehow he was not able to accept the fact that the red colour of the peacock was a natural colour. He looked at the courtier and found him to be smiling cunningly. It didn't take him time to understand that the courtier had played some trick on the King. And that was more than enough. The very next day Tenali Ramakrishna searched out the colour specialist, who had charged merely one hundred gold coins for painting in red the feathers of the peacock. That artist lived at the outskirts of the capital of Vijayanagar, and was of a very carefree type of nature.

Tenali Ramakrishna arranged to get four peacocks and got their feathers painted in red like the earlier one. And after four days he appeared at the court before the King with four red peacocks, and said, "My Lord! My colleague had to spend thirty thousand gold coins to get one red peacock, whereas, I have had to spend only four hundred gold coins to get four such red peacocks. Here are they."

King Krishna Dev Rai looked at the peacocks with great surprise, and then looked at Tenali Ramakrishna and the artist with a questioning expression.

The Courtier, who had given the red peacock to the King for thirty thousand gold coins, became nervous to see the artist with Tenali Ramakrishna. Given a chance, he would have run away from the court. But where could he go. The situation was such. The artist who had come with Tenali Ramakrishna was the same, who had painted the first peacock in red colour.

The King ordered the four peacocks to be sent to the royal garden. He then asked, "Tenali Ramakrishna! what is the matter?"

"My Lord! If there is anyone who deserves to be rewarded for these rare peacocks in such a strange colour, it is this artist. If you are really pleased to see the beauty of these peacocks, it is this artist who should be rewarded," saying this Tenali ramakrishna narrated the whole thing in detail to the King and made him aware of the truth.

Coming to know that he had been cheated by his own courtier, King Krishna Dev Rai became terribly angry. He, with immediate effect, suspended the courtier for two months, and awarded a punishment of ten thousand gold coins to him apart from the orders to deposit the thirty thousand gold coins in the royal treasure that had been paid to him.

The artist was given a handsome reward and Tenali Ramakrishna was honoured for his loyality.

❑ ❑

18

A STRANGE PRESENT

Once an emissary from the neighbouring Kingdom arrived at the court of King Krishna Dev Rai. Apart from the message sent by his King, he had also brought lots of presents for him. He was given a warm welcome in Vijayanagar. After a sojourn of three days, when he prepared to leave, King Krishna Dev Rai said, "We wish to present you with something—you may ask for anything of your choice."

The emissary was very witty and clever. He had heard a lot about Tenali Ramakrishna. This was an opportune time for him to get a

present and test the wits of Tenali Ramakrishna as well. He said, "My Lord! Diamonds, pearls, gold and silver are of no value to me. If you really wish, you may kindly give me something that would remain with me under all circumstances."

King Krishna Dev Rai was not able to decide as to what the emissary should be presented with. He looked at his courtiers with a hope that they would be able to suggest to him something. But none of the courtiers could come out with any kind of suggestion. Then he looked at Tenali Ramakrishna as the last resort. He understood what the King wanted. He rose from his seat, bowed before him with respect, and said, "My Lord! The item of the present will go with him when he leaves in the afternoon."

Tenali Ramakrishna suggested that the farewell party of the emissary may be arranged in the open at the time of his departure in the afternoon. It was bright sun in the open outside the palace building.

Meanwhile, all the items of presents were ordered to be kept in the chariot of the emissary.

Then King Krishna Dev Rai turned towards Tenali Ramakrishna and said, "Where is that item of the present that you propose to give to the emissary, which would remain with him under all circumstances?"

Tenali Ramakrishna laughed and said, "My Lord! That item has already been given and at present it is with him. Only thing is that he is not able to see it. Please ask him to look behind and see.

The emissary immediately looked back and said, "Where is it Tenali Ramakrishna Ji? I don't see anything."

"Honourable guest! Look behind and see carefully. Aren't you able to see your own shadow? It is this shadow which always remain with a person; in suffering and in delight; no one can snatch it from you, nor can anyone steal it. It has always been with you; only you were not aware of it."

The King smiled.

The emissary said, "Tenali Ramakrishna Ji! You are great indeed. King Krishna Dev Rai is fortunate to have a capable person like you at his court. It was only to test your wits and wisdom that I had asked for so strange a thing and I can say with pride that you have answered me suitably."

Tenali Ramakrishna didn't say anything. He simply smiled.

Later, after the emissary left, King Krishna Dev Rai spoke generously about Tenali Ramakrishna with a lot of praise for him. He also rewarded him sumptuously for his wits and wisdom.

❏ ❏

19

KILLJOY AND A GREATER KILLJOY

It was famous about Sukhdev, a subject of Vijayanager Kingdom, that one who sees his face early in the morning is sure to have a very bad day, and won't be able to get food throughout the day. Gradually this information reached the ears of King Krishna Dev Rai also. The King thought that he should test it himself, and if the information was true, he should not allow such a person to live in his kingdom.

Sukhdev was brought at the court. He was extended great hospitality by the King himself and then at night he ordered Sukhdeva's bed also to be arranged in his bedroom.

Early in the morning, the King, just after leaving his bed, went to the bed of Sukhdev, saw his face, enquired his well-being, and got busy in his daily routine.

Somehow the King got so entangled into something very complicated that he could not have his breakfast. He had to slip his lunch also, as, just as he was going to have his lunch, he was informed that the queen had become suddenly very unwell, and wanted to see him. Her condition became so serious that he had to miss his dinner also.

The King began thinking—'It's so inauspicious to see the face of this man early in the morning that a king like me, who has everything at his beck and call, had to miss his breakfast, lunch and dinner altogether. Such a person should not be allowed to live another day. He is a real killjoy.'

He immediately called his soldiers and ordered them to hang Sukhdev till death next evening in the presence of his subjects.

The soldiers immediately arrested Sukhdev and imprisoned him. By morning the news spread like wildfire that ill-omened Sukhdev was going to be hanged till death in the evening as ordered by King Krishna Dev Rai.

The news reached the ears of Tenali Ramakrishna also, and within the twinkling of an eye, he understood the whole thing. He immediately went and visited hapless Sukhdev in the prison. Poor Sukhdev narrated the whole sequence of happenings to him with tears rolling down his cheeks. He was pained to tell how the King himself had invited and honoured him and then ordered him to be hanged till death. He said, "Sir, I was under the impression that our King is judicious and justice-loving, but now I feel that it is otherwise."

Saying this Sukhdev began sobbing. He again said, "Sir, where am I at fault? Being inauspicious or auspicious is all God's decision. What any human being can do about it? Please help me, or else, my children will be orphaned. I have already lost my wife."

"Don't worry, Sukhdev!" said Tenali Ramakrishna, "Do exactly as I say," saying this he began whispering something in the ear of Sukhdev.

"Could you follow what I said?" asked Tenali Ramakrishna.

"Yes, I shall do exactly as you have suggested to me," said Sukhdev.

Tenali Ramakrishna took leave of him and went away.

The soldiers came in the evening and said, "Sukhdev! The King wants to know if you have any last wish."

"Jailor!" said Sukhdev fearlessly, "My last wish is to tell the subjects of this kingdom that I am a killjoy; I am so ill-omened that anyone who sees my face early in the morning, is sure to miss his breakfast, lunch and dinner altogether; he will not get a grain even to put in his mouth; but our King is a greater killjoy. He is so ill-starred that I saw his face yesterday, early in the morning, and I am under the orders of being hanged today."

"What nonsense?" said the jailor popping out his eyes angrily, "Are you aware of what you are saying? If our King comes to know about it..."

"Then what?" said Sukhdev, "Is there any punishment greater than capital punishment? Jailor! Please go and make the King aware of my last wish."

The jailor along with some soldiers went almost running to the King and conveyed the last wish of Sukhdev to him. King Krishna Dev Rai was taken aback to know his last wish. He ordered, "I cancel his capital punishment with immediate effect; go and bring him to me right now."

The soldiers went and brought Sukhdev before the King. He motioned to him to sit by his side, and then asked with great affection—

"Sukhdev! I want to know the truth. Tell me, how this bright idea flashed across your mind?"

"My Lord! Such bright ideas don't flash across the minds of fools like us. I had lost all my mental equilibrium after hearing about the award of capital punishment to me. May God bless Tenali Ramakrishna Ji, who offered his valuable suggestions to me and got me out of this situation.

"Oh," said the King. First it came like a shock to him, and then he became normal and said, "Great is Tenali Ramakrishna who saved an innocent person from capital punishment."

King Krishna Dev Rai gave a lot of gold coins to Sukhdev and bade him farewell.

❑ ❑

20

A COMPROMISE

For the last so many years King Krishna Dev Rai had been estranged from his neighbouring king. Many times it had happened that the armies of both the kingdoms had come face to face with each other. The position was no better and there was a lot of tension on both the sides, when a courtier came and began telling the King that Tenali Ramakrishna, whom he trusted most, was, in fact, a traitor. The courtier had taken advantage of isolation when King Krishna Dev Rai was having a stroll in his royal garden early in the morning.

"What did you say?" King Krishna Dev Rai looked at the courtier in disbelief and said, "Are you aware of what you are saying?"

"My Lord!" said the courtier, "I can dare bring the bitter truth to your knowledge only when you promise to spare my life after coming to know of the fact.

King Krishna Dev Rai thought for a moment and then said, "All right! Now come out with whatever you have to say."

"My lord! There is great rumour in the air that our Tenali Ramakrishna ji is an agent and informer of your enemy. Every secret matter discussed at your court reaches the ears of your enemy; that too in minute details."

Once again Krishna Dev Rai lost his temper and began shouting at the courtier.

"My Lord! This is what I was scared of. It seems you are under his hypnotic effect. And this precisely is the reason why no one of us could dare bring the truth to your knowledge. You cannot hear anything against him, My lord."

"It's a matter of individual belief My Lord. I am just as confident of my informer as you are confident of Tenali Ramakrishna. I don't believe in entering into any controversy before making sure of my statement. I have tested my information from all angles and then only dared bring it before you."

Seeing the firmness of the courtier, King Krishna Dev Rai was compelled to think that the information given by the courtier had some solid basis. He thought for some time and then said, "All right! I shall have the matter investigated secretly. And if Tenali Ramakrishna is found guitly, he will be awarded suitable punishment for treachery."

The courtier saluted him and left.

King Krishna Dev Rai summoned Tenali Ramakrishna to his presence as soon as the courtier left, and asked a straight question—

"Tenali Ramakrishna! I have been informed that you are involved in treachery and are hand in glove with my neighbour king who is my enemy. I have also been informed that you have been supplying secret information to him. Is it true?"

Tenali Ramakrishna was stunned to hear this. He remained in that position for quite some time wearing a blank look on his face. The blame was of such magnitude that he was totally nonplussed. He was silent; he couldn't say anything.

"Your silence is the proof of your treachery; is the proof of the correctness of the information given to me. You are a traitor," said King Krishna Dev Rai angrily.

"My Lord!" Tenali Ramakrishna's eyes brimmed with tears, "What are you..."

But King Krishna Dev Rai wouldn't let him speak. He said, "If you have so much sympathy for my enemy, go and live in his kingdom. Leave this kingdom at once."

The King had made him aware of his final decision.

"My Lord! So simple a punishment for so big a crime?" said Tenali Ramakrishna in a choked voice.

"Taking into consideration the past services rendered and the status of the post held by you, it is deemed fit to award you a minor

punishment only—had the crime of the same magnitude been committed by someone else, I would have had his body cut into pieces and offered to kites and crows," said King Krishna Dev Rai boiling with anger.

Tenali Ramakrishna listened to his final decision quietly and bowed before the King respectfully, and without uttering a single word, he left the place and went away.

Next day—

The news spread like wildfire all over Vijayanagar that Tenali Ramakrishna had been exiled by the King. The jealous courtiers were filled with boundless happiness. Now they began thinking of enhancing their powers and getting promotions.

Meanwhile, Tenali Ramakrishna, exiled from his motherland, reached the capital of the kingdom of the enemy king, and met him. He described the good qualities of the enemy king and his kingdom in couplets. The King was not acquainted with him. He asked him his identity. The enemy king was extremely pleased to know the identity of Tenali Ramakrishna. He had heard a lot about him. He ordered a royal welcome and hospitality in his honour.

After having met all the formalities, the enemy king made Tenali Ramakrishna sit by his side and said, "Tenali Ramakrishna Ji! Your King considers me his enemy, then how is it that you came to my kingdom without any fear. Didn't you think that something untoward could have happened to you in my kingdom. Or is it that you have come with some message from your King?"

"King! You are an erudite scholar; you are gentle and virtuous; you are extremely powerful and a capable administrator; you are a well-wisher of your subjects. My King too possesses just as many qualities. He doesn't consider you a foe, he considers you a friend. My King has sent me to you to remove the misunderstanding of prolonged enmity between him and you."

"What did you say?" the enemy king was startled, "King Krishna Dev Rai has himself sent you to me and he considers me his friend? But my spies say that he is preparing to launch an attack on us."

"King! I can only say that this is the ignorance of spies. It seems there is some grave misunderstanding between us, and the armies of both the kingdoms are standing face to face with each other at the borders. King! History is witness to wars that have fetched no positive results except destruction and loss of human lives. And for this very reason my King has sent me to you to find out the reason why you are so much willing to have a war with him."

"But this is not true," said the enemy king, "I, in no way, want a war. Seeing your army at the borders, I too had to send my army in self-defence. Now you say that King Krishna Dev Rai doesn't want a war—but how to believe that he doesn't want a war and wants to make friends with me."

"In that case," said Tenali Ramakrishna, "send your emissary to Vijayanagar with a few presents and a compromise letter. I shall also give a letter to your emissary. If King Krishna Dev Rai accepts your presents, you should believe that he is willing to make friends with you, and if he declines to accept, I shall be ready to take any punishments awarded by you."

"But this will be considered a compromise from my side. This will rather be taken as a cowardice on my part. People would think that I have sent the compromise letter out of fear," said the enemy king.

"No, there isn't anything like cowardice in it. Anything done for the well-being of the subjects and for maintaining peace is never considered shameful," said Tenali Ramakrishna.

The enemy king realised the truth in what he said, and the very next day he sent an emissary to Vijayanagar with lots of valuable presents and a compromise letter.

Meanwhile, in two days, King Krishna Dev Rai had found out the real truth and also discovered how the cunning courtiers had played a dirty trick on him and Tenali Ramakrishna. Coming to know that Tenali Ramakrishna was not guilty, he had decided that he would award severe punishment to the guilty courtiers. But right now he was restless about his well-being and whereabouts.

On the third day, as soon as the emissary arrived at his court with lots of valuable presents and a compromise letter, and narrated the matter to him, he became extremely happy. With a lot of praise for the wisdom of Tenali Ramakrishna in his heart, he immediately sent a minister to the neighbour king with lots of valuable presents, and requested in a letter addressed to the king that Tenali Ramakrishna may be sent back with honour.

And King Krishna Dev Rai embraced Tenali Ramakrishna with great love, when he returned to Vijayanagar.

The jealous courtiers who had hatched a conspiracy against Tenali Ramakrishna had to fight shy of their shameful acts. King Krishna Dev Rai was in favour of awarding severe punishment to those courtiers, but

Tenali Ramakrishna requested him not to do so, and said, "My Lord! Had they not hatched such conspiracy, a chance for a compromise with your neighbour king would not have arisen—you should be grateful to them.

The jealous courtiers were ashamed when they saw Tenali Ramakrishna counteracting in this manner.

❑ ❑

21

HOW MANY CROWS

King Krishna Dev Rai at times, used to pose difficult problems and awkward questions before Tenali Ramakrishna in order to tease him and enjoy the situation. But Tenali Ramakrishna was so shrewd that he would give a witty reply, and the King wouldn't be able to say anything.

On one such day the King asked him, "Tenali Ramakrishna! can you tell me the number of crows in my kingdom?"

"Yes, I can, My Lord," came a quick reply from Tenali Ramakrishna.

"But I want the exact number," said the King.

"My Lord! I shall give you the exact number," said Tenali Ramakrishna.

"And if you fail to tell me the exact number, you will be awarded a capital punishment," said the King with a smile.

"I take the challenge, My Lord," said Tenali Ramakrishna fearlessly.

The courtiers could well imagine that Tenali Ramakrishna was going to get into deep trouble. They were sure that counting of birds was an impossible task.

"All right! I allow you two days time. On the third day you have to tell me the exact number of crows in my kingdom," said the King.

On the third day Tenali Ramakrishna attended the court. King Krishna Dev Rai looked at him and asked, "Have you counted the crows in my kingdom?"

Tenali Ramakrishna rose from his seat and said, "My Lord! There are one lakh fifty six thousand nine hundred and twelve crows in all in your kingdom."

"Is this true?" asked the King in bewilderment.

"My Lord! You may have them counted by someone else, in case you have any doubts," said Tenali Ramakrishna.

"And if I have them recounted and find your number to be less or more, then...," said the King.

"My Lord!" said Tenali Ramakrishna, "First of all, there won't be any difference in the number given by me, and if at all there happens to be a difference in the number given by me, it will have some genuine reason."

"And what's that genuine reason?" asked the King.

"If the number increases," said Tenali Ramakrishna, "it would mean that some relatives of the crows of our kingdom may have come to see them; and if the number decreases, it would mean that some crows of our kingdom may have gone to see their relatives in some other kingdom. Otherwise, the number given by me is absolutely correct."

King Krishna Dev Rai had no reply.

The jealous courtiers were once again irritated to see that Tenali Ramakrishna had once again come out of a difficult situation without any problem.

King Krishna Dev rewarded him handsomely for his wits and wisdom.

❑ ❑

22

WHO IS MORE SHREWD

One day King Krishna Dev Rai asked Tenali Ramakrishna, "Among the human beings who are the most cowardly and foolish ones, and who are the most shrewd ones?"

Tenali Ramakrishna cast a look at the spiritual preceptor of the King and then said, "My Lord! Brahmins are the most cowardly and foolish ones, and Vaishyas (Businessmen) are the most shrewd ones."

"What is it that you are saying, Tenali Ramakrishna? Brahmins are educated and erudite scholars. How can a businessman stand in comparison with a Brahmin?" said the King.

"My Lord! I can prove my point," Tenali Ramakrishna was adamant.

"How?" asked the King curiously.

"I shall prove the truth of what I have said tomorrow at the court.

Next day when the court was in full swing, Tenali Ramakrishna called the spiritual preceptor to him and said, "Sir, the King has entrusted me with a job and given me complete freedom to perform it. In connection with this job, I can punish or reward anyone at my will," and then turning towards the King he said, "Am I correct, My Lord?"

"Yes," said the King, "I have given special rights to him to perform a particular type of job."

All the courtiers were surprised as to what kind of job had the King entrusted him with that he had been conferred a right to punish also. And then why is it that Tenali Ramakrishna is telling the spiritual preceptor about it. "There must be something fishy," thought the courtiers.

The spiritual preceptor too was very much confused. He said, "What you say is correct, Tenali Ramakrishna, but why did you call me here and then why is it that you are telling me all this?"

"Don't get nervous, sir!" said Tenali Ramakrishna, "In fact our King needs your tuft, and you will be paid to your demand for this."

The spiritual preceptor was in a very strange state of predicament. "How whimsical is our King? Is a tuft something that should be taken away from someone?" thought he to himself. He was looking at the King nervously.

But the King was sitting without any reaction.

"What are you thinking, sir?" said Tenali Ramakrishana, "Do you refuse to give your tuft to the King?"

"No, no, Tenali Ramakrishna Ji!" spoke the spiritual preceptor falteringly, "The order of the King is above everything in the world. But this tuft of mine is symbolic of my erudition and status."

"Oh!" Tenali Ramakrishna said tauntingly, "so your status is above the wish of your King?" Then he admonished him saying, "Lifelong you have been taken care of by the King, and today you are refusing to give so smiple a thing to him. Do you know the head of yours which sports this tuft can be ordered to be cut off by the King, but our King is very judicious and justice-loving; he doesn't want to harm you in any manner. Otherwise, he could have straightaway ordered to decapitate you and taken away your tuft."

The spiritual preceptor began trembling with fear. It had become clear to him that Tenali Ramakrishna had posed such a problem before him that it had become impossible for him to get out of it.

"Five gold coins will do for my tuft," said the spiritual preceptor haltingly.

He was given five gold coins immediately. Then a barber was asked to shave off his tuft.

Now Tenali Ramakrishna summoned the most famous businessman of the town. He too had a long tuft, rather he was popularly known as 'Chotiwala'.

"What is it that you want of me, sir?" asked the businessman.

Tenali Ramakrishna said, "Listen 'chotiwala'! Due to certain important reasons our King needs your long tuft."

"O great Tenali Ramakrishna Ji! Everything that I have belongs to our King only. He may have it any time he wants. But, Sir! Please keep in mind that I am an extremely poor man," said the businessman.

"You will be suitably paid for your tuft," said Tenali Ramakrishna.

"Hey, hey, hey...it is all the judiciousness of our King, but...simpered the businessman.

"'But' what?"

"Sir, in fact, it is this tuft with which I manage everything. I spent five thousand gold coins in the marriage of my daughter only to save the prestige of this tuft. Last year I spent five thousand gold coins after the death of my father. It is because of this tuft that I can borrow ten to twenty thousand gold coins from the market whenever I need," said the businessman.

"You mean to say that the value of your tuft is twenty five thousand gold coins," said Tenali Ramakrishna with a smile.

"What more can I say, sir?" said the businessman.

"All right! you will get it," saying this Tenali Ramakrishna ordered him to be paid twenty five thousand gold coins.

Having received the gold coins, the businessman sat down to have his tuft shaved off.

And then, as soon as the barber put his hand on his tuft, 'chotiwala' shouted, "O cunning barber! Have reverence for this tuft. Don't you know that this our King's tuft now?"

"What did you say?" King Krishna Dev Rai became very angry to hear him speaking thus. "You fool! How dare you insult me? Throw him out of the court immediately."

The businessman immediately picked up his bag of twenty five thousand gold coins and ran away from there.

Tenali Ramakrishna burst into laughter and said, "Now it must have become clear to you, My Lord, as to who is foolish and who is shrewd. The spiritual preceptor got his tuft shaved off for five gold coins only, and that shrewd businessman took away twenty five thousand gold coins and saved his tuft also from getting shaved off."

"You had correctly said Tenali Ramakrishna that businessmen are shrewd," said King Krishna Dev Rai.

❑ ❑

23

CRAFTY MOVE OF THE SPIRITUAL PRECEPTOR

There were many courtiers who were extremely jealous of Tenali Ramakrishna, but the spiritual preceptor of the King was a bit too jealous of him. Especially the day when Tenali Ramakrishna had one hundred and seven Brahmins seared with hot iron rods by his servants. He always kept planning ways to get him thrown out of the palace or let him down in the eyes of King Krishna Dev Rai.

Ultimately one day an idea came across the mind of the spiritual preceptor. During those days the lazy and foolish brother of the Queen had come. One day the spiritual preceptor insinuated the brother of the Queen that Tenali Ramakrishna was being given undue importance by the King. He neither had any special capability nor did he have any virtues. The honourable position which Tenali Ramakrishna was holding was not deserved by him.

The foolish brother of the Queen was fully convinced that he was more capable than Tenali Ramakrishna. He went to the Queen and spoke his mind to her. The Queen tried her level best to explain to him that Tenali Ramakrishna had not reached that honourable post just like that; he had performed great deeds to reach that height, but her foolish brother refused to listen to any logics.

He was insisting—

"Come what may, I must get that honourable seat. Tenali Ramakrishna must be thrown out of the palace; and it is only you who can make it possible."

The Queen had great regards for Tenali Ramakrishna, but a brother is after all a brother, she had to honour his feelings also. In the evening when the King arrived the Queen demanded straightaway that Tenali Ramakrishna be thrown out of his place.

The King was greatly surprised, but he didn't pay much attention to what she said. The Queen understood that it wasn't so easy as she had thought it to be. She decided that she would have to cling to some other ruse next day.

Next day when the King arrived, the Queen was lying motionless in her bed. The King was astonished to see that she didn't even welcome him.

He said, "Queen! What's the problem with you? why are you so silent? Has someone hurt your feelings?"

The Queen spoke with tearful eyes, "Is it that you cannot do anything for me?"

"Queen!" said King Krishna Dev Rai, "Tell me, if there is anything that I have not done for you."

"Had I not asked you to displace Tenali Ramakrishna and appoint my brother in his place," said the Queen in a choked voice.

King Krishna Dev Rai had not come mentally prepared for this question. Moreover, he was well aware of the foolishness of his brother-in-law. Even the Queen was aware of it, but the wiles of a female was getting the better of her. And so it was necessary to make things clear to her. The King thought for a while and then said, "Look Queen! there will be great unrest and agitation among my subjects if I displace Tenali Ramakrishna without assigning any genuine reason. I shall have to look for a reasonable cause before I dicide to displace him."

"You shall have to make efforts to get some suitable reason," said the Queen.

"Efforts? What efforts?" asked the King.

"Yes, My Lord!" said the Queen, "Do as I say. Leave this place and return under a pretension of anger with me. Go to the court and tell Tenali Ramakrishna that he should come here and take me to you. And warn him that if he could not take me to your presence, he would be displaced. He will come to me but I shall not budge from my place. And that will become enough of a reason to displace him.

The King smiled furtively thinking that the Queen thought Tenali Ramakrishna to be a child. He didn't say anything and agreed to act as directed by the Queen.

The very next day, the news of the Queen's anger with the King, spread like wildfire. The King repeated the words of the Queen when Tenali Ramakrishna went to meet him. He was alarmed. He was quick to understand that there was something fishy. He came out, explained something to his trusted man and set out towards the palace of the Queen.

Just when Tenali Ramakrishna was enquiring about her well-being, his trusted man came and without any preamble, he said, "You are bothering yourself unnecessarily. The King is adamant. He has taken a firm decision that he is going to bring another wife. Tenali Ramakrishna Ji! Things have gone out of our hand now."

"Oh," Tenali Ramakrishna sighed a sigh. Suddenly he became very serious as if everything had been ruined.

The Queen became suspicious. She thought to herself—"Is it that the King has really become angry with me? Otherwise, what is it all about another marriage?" She asked Tenali Ramakrishna, "Tell me, What's all this? What am I hearing?"

Tenali Ramakrishna said, "In fact, Queen Sahiba! The King is terribly angry with you. What did you say to him that the matter has gone that far? He was telling me that he doesn't like any kind of interference in his administration. Perhaps you have put some demand before him, which is much against his will, and he is so angry with you, that he has decided to bring another wife."

"No, no, he cannot do that. I shall go and talk to him; I shall convince him that I shall not interfere in his administrative matters in future. Tenali Ramakrishna Ji! Please take me to the King immediately.

Tenali Ramakrishna was already looking for this kind of oppportunity. He immediately took the Queen to King Krishna Dev Rai. He had already explained to her in the way, her next course of action. So the Queen immediately apologized before the King and said, "My Lord! I

152

take a vow that I shall not interfere in your administrative matters in future. Please forgive me this time."

King Krishna Dev Rai was greatly surprised. He thought to himself— "What is this all? She had decided that she won't move from her place; and what I see is that she has not only come running before me, she is seeking an apology also. He said, "Queen! It seems Tenali Ramakrishna has fooled you."

"Please don't say that, My Lord," said the Queen, "Tenali Ramakrishna Ji is rather trying to settle our differences. It was my foolishness that I was trying to get him displaced unnecessarily. Now I apologize before you. Please promise that you won't bring another wife."

Hearing this, King Krishna Dev Rai roared with laughter. Then he told the Queen how strange was Tenali Ramakrishna. It wasn't easy to punish him. He said, "Now it must have become clear to you why he cannot be replaced by anyone."

24

MARRIAGE OF THE ROYAL WELL

Once King Krishna Dev Rai became very angry with Tenali Ramakrishna for some unknown reason. The King removed him from his post and asked him to leave his kingdom.

Tenali Ramakrishna bowed before the King respectfully and without waiting another moment, he left. He did not tell anyone where he was going. The courtiers who were jealous of him took a sigh of relief. They happily congratulated each other.

But King Krishna Dev Rai, who had become very much used to the jests of Tenali Ramakrishna, began missing him. Now he was feeling sorry to have exiled him. He wanted him to come back. But the greatest problem was that none knew where he had gone; not even his wife.

During these days the court proceedings did continue, but in such a monotonous way that one day the King could not take his absence any more. He sent his chosen spies in all the directions, but all in vain.

"Where is my Tenali Ramakrishna, my court jester, my heart; where is he," the eyes of the King brimmed with tear.

Things had gone so bad without Tenali Ramakrishna that the King had stopped taking interest in the court proceedings also. He would think of one ruse, then another, but nothing would seem practical. One day he was sitting in his throne and thinking of some possible way to get his court jester back. Suddenly a bright idea flashed across his mind. He immediately ordered one of his ministers to circulate letters among all the Kings of the neighbouring kingdoms, saying that King Krishna Dev Rai had arranged to get his royal well married and that all the kings were expected to send the wells of their kingdoms to attend the marriage procession and grace the occasion.

This strange kind of invitation was circulated and all the kings were simply puzzled to read the message. King Krishna Dev Rai was a powerful King and so it was obligatory for the kings to respond. But the invitation was such that all the kings were at their wits end. With the result, none answered his invitation.

King Krishna Dev Rai was again on the verge of losing all his hopes, when one fine morning he received an answer from his neighbouring kingdom, which said—

"The wells of my kingdom are willing to go to your kingdom, but they expect that all the wells of your kingdom should be present at the entrance of your capital to welcome them."

This was indeed a very shrewd reply. King Krishna Dev Rai was sure that it could be none other than Tenali Ramakrishna to have sent such a shrewd reply. He became very happy, and immediately sent an emissary with lots of valuable presents to the King of that kingdom, requesting him to send Tenali Ramakrishna back with royal honour.

Tenali Ramakrishna returned. King Krishna Dev Rai was waiting for him with open arms. He immediately embraced him and said—

"O Tenali Rama! You don't know how much we have missed you and your jests during all these days of your absence.

❑ ❑

25

AWARDING PUNISHMENT

One day when King Krishna Dev Rai was in a very good and light mood, Tenali Ramakrishna took a promise from him that if he ever committed a mistake or there was a serious lapse on his part, knowingly or unknowingly, he should have a right to select his own judges to award punishment to him.

King Krishna Dev Rai agreed to it and said, "Though I permit you to select your own judges when required, it should not become a precedent for others."

One day Tenali Ramakrishna said something to the King, while performing jests at the court, that did not suit his status. The King became very angry with him and said that he must be awarded some major punishment.

Tenali Ramakrishna reminded him of his promise and said, "My Lord! As per the word given by you, I have a right to request you to appoint judges of my choice."

The King remembered his promise and said, "Yes, I do remember my promise and I allow you to select your own judges."

Then Tenali Ramakrishna selected five cobblers of the town to be appointed as his judges. The King was simply surprised. He said, "What justice do you expect these cobblers to do? Isn't it foolish? Shouldn't you have selected some educated persons to be appointed as your judges? But it's your choice anyway."

And finally, according to Tenali Ramakrishna's choice, five cobblers were appointed to give a hearing to his case.

Tenali Ramakrishna explained his lapse to the cobblers and requested them to award a suitable punishment for the lapse committed by him.

The cobblers contemplated and discussed the issue among themselves and then one of them said, "My Lord! the lapse on the part of Tenali Ramakrishna Ji is of a serious nature. He should be made to pay a fine of one hundred gold coins."

The second cobbler said, "But this is too big an amount. Just think, payment of such a huge amount will make his wife and children suffer," saying this the second cobbler decreased the amount of fine by twenty gold coins.

But the third cobbler was of the view that even an amount of eighty gold coins as fine was more than too much. And he brought it down to twenty gold coins.

The amount of twenty gold coins, as fine, was also not found to be adequate by the fourth and fifth cobblers and they considered it a bit on the higher side.

Anyway...after a great deal of discussion, it was decided by them, that Tenali Ramakrishna should be made to pay as fine an amount of five gold coins.

King Krishna Dev Rai was quick to understand how clever Tenali Ramakrishna had been to manoeuvre the judgement in his favour.

Having awarded the punishment the cobblers went away, and Tenali Ramakrishna was smiling furtively.

"Tenali Ramakrishna! What made you elect to choose cobblers to be appointed as judges," asked the King with a smile.

"My Lord!" said Tenali Ramakrishna, "People generally judge the economic status of others by their own status; and that's precisely the reason why I elected to choose these poor cobblers as my judges. Had I selected some minister or courtier to be appointed as my judge, he would have fined me not less than at least one thousand gold coins; whereas this amount was simply beyond imagination for these cobblers."

King Krishna Dev Rai felt pity for the poverty-stricken cobblers of his kingdom and also, was very much pleased to see his court jester's wit and wisdom.

❏ ❏

26

GOD'S MESSAGE

Once King Krishna Dev Rai decided to have a big temple of Lord Shiva made in his kingdom. He ordered one of his ministers to find a suitable place for the temple.

The minister chose a piece of land near a nearby forest for the construction of the temple.

The work started with immediate effect.

During the cleaning of that place, an old ruined temple of Lord Shiva was found, where after excavation a life-size golden statue of Lord Shiva emerged.

Seeing the statue made of solid gold allured the minister and he quietly sent it home.

Among the labours doing the excavation work there were some men of Tenali Ramakrishna also. They immediately informed him about it.

Tenali Ramakrishna kept mum about it and began waiting for the opportune time.

Meanwhile, after performing all the religious rites and worshipping the land, the construction work of the temple of Lord Shiva started.

One day when the court proceedings were going on, King Krishna Dev Rai began discussing with the courtiers and ministers about the type of statue to be made for the temple.

All the courtiers and ministers began giving their opinions about it.

King Krishna Dev Rai couldn't reach any definite conclusion and left it for the next day to be discussed at the court.

Next day when the court was in full swing, suddenly a sage with long hair and beard was seen entering the court. The King rose from his throne and welcoming the sage with honour, he offered him a seat.

"King!" said the sage, "I am the messenger of Lord Shiva. I have come here to get you out of your problem."

"Message from Lord Shiva...," the King was extremely excited, "Maharaj! Please let me know without delay. What message has Lord Shiva sent for me?"

"King!" said the sage, "Seeing your concern about the statue of Lord Shiva, Lord Shiva has himself sent a life-size golden statue for the temple. At present the statue is lying in the house of your minister. Get it from his house and have it consecrated in the temple...victory to Lord Shiva," and with these words the sage went away.

King Krishna Dev Rai looked at the minister. And the minister was already nervous thinking as to how the sage came to know about the golden statue lying in his house. But now, since the fact had been revealed before the King, he thought it better to admit it.

Suddenly the King realised something and looked around. Tenali Ramakrishna was not to be seen anywhere.

And before he could solve the puzzle, Tenali Ramakrishna was seen coming.

Everyone laughed to see him coming. One courtier said, "My Lord! He is the one who had come as a sage. He changed his clothes and removed his long hair and beard, but forgot to take out the string of beads.

Once again there was a roar of laughter.

"Now the construction of the temple will take place under the supervision of Tenali Ramakrishna," said King Krishna Dev Rai.

❏ ❏

27

MAGIC SHOW WITH CLOSED EYES

Once a magician visited Vijayanagar. He was more accomplished in performing his shows by sleight of hand than performing black magics. He visited the King also at his court and showed many magic tricks. He transformed pebbles into gold coins. He also beheaded himself before the King.

He was applauded by everyone for his great show. Being applauded thus filled him with ego. He said in a loud voice, "My Lord! Is there any magician in the whole of your kingdom who can compete with me?"

King Krishna Dev Rai couldn't say anything, as indeed there was none in the whole of his kingdom who could compete with that magician.

Seeing the King not able to take his challenge the magician was filled more with pride. He again said, "My Lord! I challenge and am ready to offer my head to anyone in your kingdom who can defeat me in performing magic tricks."

There was absolute silence at the court. Neither the King nor the courtiers were able to say anything. But Tenali Ramakrishna found it greatly insulting. He could bear no more of his boasting. He rose from his seat and said, "O magician! Don't talk rubbish. I find it irritating to see your pomposity. Now take a challenge from me. I challenge, you cannot perform the miracle with your eyes open that I can perform with my eyes closed."

King Krishna Dev Rai was extremely pleased to see Tenali Ramakrishna throwing a challenge at the magician. He had full confidence in him. He was aware that if Tenali Ramakrishna had taken the challenge, he would definitely do something to kill the pride of the magician and save his prestige.

But, poor magician was not aware of the capabilities of Tenali Ramakrishna. So he again spoke in a loud tone, "What nonsense are you talking? What kind of miracle is it that you can perform with your closed eyes, and I cannot perform with my open eyes? All right! If this is so, show me your miracle, and if I lose, I shall offer my head to you."

I am not talking nonsense, I am talking correct sense," said Tenali Ramakrishna confidently, "Wait for some time and I shall show one," saying this he whispered something in the ear of his servant who was standing near him.

The servant went away. He returned after some time with a cup in his hand which was full of red chilly powder. Tenali Ramakrishna took a handful of red chilly powder and poured it on his closed eyes. Then wiping his eyelids with a piece of cloth he said—

"Now either you perform this miracle with open eyes or accept your defeat."

The magician was already nonplussed to see what he had done. He knew, repeating the same performance with open eyes would mean losing his sight altogether. It was an impossible task.

Throwing the challenge at the magician, Tenali Ramakrishna went away to wash his face. The magician was standing motionless in his place.

Tenali Ramakrishna returned and repeated his challenge.

The magician stepped forward, bowed before Tenali Ramakrishna and said, "Sir, I accept my defeat. You can have my head."

"I don't want your head, magician. I can forgive you but you shall have to promise that you will never let your ego have the better of you in future," said Tenali Ramakrishna.

"I promise," said the magician.

The magician collected all his items of magic tricks, bowed before the King and went away.

King Krishna Dev Rai became very happy to see the wit and wisdom of Tenali Ramakrishna and rewarded him handsomely.

28

A TRIBUTE

One day Tenali Ramakrishna was bitten by a poisonous snake. It was a deadly one and there was no hope of Tenali Ramakrishna's survival.

At the time of death his last wish was to meet his friend—King Krishna Dev Rai. He sent someone with a message to the King that Tenali Ramakrishna was breathing his last and wanted to see the King before death.

Hearing the message from the person, the King laughed and said, "Today again he is pretending to be on deathbed. He has played the same kind of tricks earlier also to fool me. Tell him to stop cutting jokes, and come and attend the court."

"I beg your pardon, My Lord!" said the man with folded hands, "This is no joke; this is a serious message. He has been bitten by a deadly snake."

"Yes, yes, why not!" said King Krishna Dev Rai, "He had to be bitten by a deadly snake this time, because he is aware that pretending to be suffering from some strange kind of disease, is not going to work this time. I admit, he is very clever, but I am not going to be fooled by him this time. You may go now."

The man returned and informed Tenali Ramakrishna about how the King had reacted.

Tenali Ramakrishna's eyes brimmed with tears. He said in a choked voice—

"Isn't this a mockery of fate. A liar is not believed even when he tells a truth. I know, when the King comes to know about my death, he will be extremely sad. Anyway...at least I have the satisfaction at the time of my death that I remained a favourite of the King throughout my life."

And then! After some time Tenali Ramakrishna breathed his last. He wore a beautiful smile even after his death. Perhaps some happy moment of his life had struck his memory at the time of his death.

Meanwhile King Krishna Dev Rai was thinking—

"The man who had come with the message of his being on death-bed, looked quite sad. The information brought by him might have been true. Has he really been bitten by a snake? It doesn't take time for a mishappening to take place. I must go and see him."

The King, now, had a strong feeling that there was something seriously wrong. He immediately started for his house. But, alas, it was too late. Tenali Ramakrishna was no more. He had breathed his last even before the King could come and see him.

"What? Is he really no more?" King Krishna Dev Rai was momentarily taken aback. He said in a choked voice, "No, no, he is only pretending to be dead. Look, look, what kind of smile he is wearing on his face," saying this the King began shaking him madly. "Please open your eyes, Tenali Ramakrishna. Please talk to your friend. Say at least something. I know you are not dead. Jolly people like you don't die. You have made me laugh throughout your life. Now please don't leave me by making me weep. Who will make me laugh if you go away? Who will perform jests for me if you go away? Tenali Ramakrishna! Open your eyes, please open your eyes..."

And then—King Krishna Dev Rai began weeping bitterly like a child, with his head on the chest of Tenali Ramakrishna.

Everyone began consoling the King.

Next day, Tenali Ramakrishna's body was cremated with royal honour. King Krishna Dev Rai was quietly watching the smoke rising from his pyre and disappearing in the sky. His eyes were brimmed with tears. He was thinking—

"Will another Tenali Ramakrishna take birth on the earth? Never...perhaps never! Never so witty a jester would be born."

King Krishna Dev Rai Kept thinking and tears continued rolling down his cheeks. Even those courtiers, who were staunch opponents of Tenali Ramakrishna, had tears in their eyes. All the subjects of Vijayanagar were shedding tears.

And these tears were the real tribute to the court jester of Vijayanagar.

A Treasure of Stories
Specially for CHILDREN

Big Size Illustrated

☐ 101 Stories from Panchatantra	80.00
☐ Akbar Birbal Stories	80.00
☐ The Arabian Nights	80.00
☐ 101 Stories of Grand Mother	80.00
☐ Vikram Betal	80.00
☐ 101 Stories of Grandpa	80.00
☐ Aesop's Stories	80.00
☐ Jataka Tales	80.00
☐ Ramayana	80.00
☐ Mahabharata	80.00
☐ Fair Fair Fairy Tales	80.00
☐ Best Stories for Children	80.00
☐ Selected Stories from The Holy Bible	80.00
☐ Witty Tenali Rama	80.00
☐ Chandamama Stories	80.00
☐ The World's Most Popular Folk Tales	80.00
☐ Hillariously Funny Mulla Nasrudin	80.00
☐ Hitopadesh	80.00
☐ Shekhchilli	80.00
☐ Ghost Stories	80.00
☐ World Famous Adventure Stories	80.00
☐ Stories of Talisman	80.00
☐ Horror Stories	80.00
☐ Jungle Stories	80.00
☐ Singhasana Battisi	80.00

These Stories are not only engrossing but are also full of moral and social values

MANOJ PUBLICATIONS
761, Main Road Burari, Delhi-110084.
Ph. No. : 27611116, 27611349   Fax : 27611546
Mobile : 9868112194

COMPUTER BOOKS

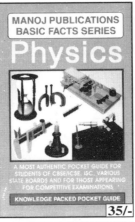

COOKERY BOOKS IN ENGLISH

Taste From Your Kitchen

● 80/- Each

- ❑ Punjabi Dishes
- ❑ Mughlai Dishes
- ❑ Soups and Sharbats
- ❑ Stuffed & Fried Vegetable
- ❑ Vegetarian Dishes
- ❑ Low Calorie Food
- ❑ Microwave Cooking
- ❑ Delicious Breakfast

- ❑ Gujrati Vyanjan
- ❑ Achaar, Chutney, Murabbe
- ❑ Dal, Curries and Pulao
- ❑ Ice Creams, Cakes & Puddings
- ❑ Chatpati Chat
- ❑ Rajasthani Vyanjan
- ❑ South Indian Dishes
- ❑ Tasty Snacks

MANOJ PUBLICATIONS

761, Main Road Burari, Delhi-110084.
Ph. No. : 27611116, 27611349   Fax : 27611546
Mobile : 9868112194

BOOK OF FATE & FORTUNE

The World famous Cheiro's Books on Palmistry and Numerology

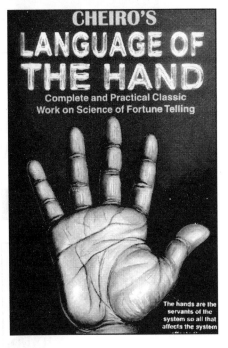

It is a well-known fact that, even if the skin be burned off the hands or removed by an acid, in a short time the lines will re-appear exactly as they were before, and the same happens to the ridges or "spirals" in the skin of the inside tips of the fingers and thumb.

In presenting this book to the public, I need then offer no other apology for so doing, than that of having been a student of this particular branch of thought for a very long period, and having proved so called theories by countless experiments and experience, I feel I am at last in a position to give to the world at large the result of such studies.

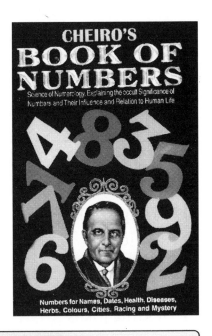

MANOJ PUBLICATIONS

761, Main Road Burari, Delhi-110084.
Ph. No. : 27611116, 27611349   Fax : 27611546
Mobile : 9868112194

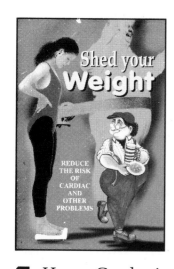

Set of
Small Size

ENGLISH
GENERAL BOOKS

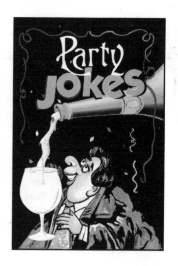

☐ Home Gardening	50.00
☐ 101 Feng Shui Tips	50.00
☐ 101 Vastu Tips	50.00
☐ Dadi Maa's Home Remedies	50.00
☐ Pregnancy & Child Care	40.00
☐ Baby Health & Child Care	40.00
☐ All About Yoga	40.00
☐ Diabetes Cause & Cure	40.00
☐ Hypertension Cause & Cure	40.00
☐ Shed Your Weight	40.00
☐ How to Increase Your Height	40.00
☐ How to Increase Sex Power	40.00

SET OF SMALL ENGLISH JOKE BOOKS

☐ Juicy Joke Book (Surendra Mohan Pathak)   50.00

☐ Midnight Jokes	30.00	☐ Superhit Jokes	30.00
☐ Party Jokes	30.00	☐ Non-Veg Jokes	30.00
☐ Naughty Jokes	30.00	☐ International Jokes	30.00
☐ Spicy Jokes	30.00	☐ SMS Jokes	30.00
☐ Tickling Jokes	30.00	☐ Internet Jokes	30.00

MANOJ PUBLICATIONS
761, Main Road Burari, Delhi-110084.
Ph. No. : 27611116, 27611349   Fax : 27611546
Mobile : 9868112194